Riley Mae
and the
Sole Fire Safari

Also by Jill Osborne

Riley Mae and the Rock Shocker Trek
Riley Mae and the Ready Eddy Rapids

Other books in the growing Faithgirlz!™ library

Bibles

The Faithgirlz! Bible
NIV Faithgirlz! Backpack Bible

Faithgirlz! Bible Studies

Secret Power of Love
Secret Power of Joy
Secret Power of Goodness
Secret Power of Grace

Fiction
From Sadie's Sketchbook

Shades of Truth (Book One)
Flickering Hope (Book Two)
Waves of Light (Book Three)
Brilliant Hues (Book Four)

Sophie's World Series

Meet Sophie (Book One)
Sophie Steps Up (Book Two)
Sophie and Friends (Book Three)
Sophie's Friendship Fiasco (Book Four)
Sophie Flakes Out (Book Five)
Sophie's Drama (Book Six)

The Lucy Series
Lucy Doesn't Wear Pink (Book One)

Lucy Out of Bounds (Book Two)

Lucy's Perfect Summer (Book Three)

Lucy Finds Her Way (Book Four)

The Girls of Harbor View
Girl Power (Book One)

Take Charge (Book Two)

Raising Faith (Book Three)

Secret Admirer (Book Four)

Boarding School Mysteries
Vanished (Book One)

Betrayed (Book Two)

Burned (Book Three)

Poisoned (Book Four)

Samantha Sanderson
Samantha Sanderson At the Movies

Samantha Sanderson On the Scene

Nonfiction

Faithgirlz Handbook

Faithgirlz Journal

Food, Faith, and Fun! Faithgirlz Cookbook

Best Party Book Ever!

Big Book of Quizzes

Real Girls of the Bible

My Beautiful Daughter

You! A Christian Girl's Guide to Growing Up

Girl Politics

Everybody Tells Me to Be Myself, but I Don't Know Who I Am

Devotions for Girls Series

No Boys Allowed

What's a Girl to Do?

Girlz Rock

Chick Chat

Shine On, Girl!

Check out www.faithgirlz.com

The Good News Shoes

Riley Mae
and the
Sole Fire Safari

BOOK THREE

Jill Osborne

ZONDERKIDZ

Riley Mae and the Sole Fire Safari
Copyright © 2014 by Jill Osborne

This title is also available as a Zondervan ebook.
Visit www.zondervan.com/ebooks

Requests for information should be addressed to:
Zonderkidz, 3900 *Sparks Drive SE, Grand Rapids, Michigan 49546*

Library of Congress Cataloging-in-Publication Data
Osborne, Jill, 1961-
    Riley Mae and the Sole Fire Safari / by Jill Osborne.
      pages cm. — (The good news shoes ; bk. 3) (Faithgirlz!)
    Summary: Although adjusting to African culture is difficult, Riley Mae grows
physically stronger and connects with Christian women and children in Kenya,
where she and her Swiftriver friends hope to escape their enemies, until a
misstep leads to big trouble.
    ISBN 978-0-310-74283-8 (softcover) — ISBN 978-0-310-74286-9 (epub)
    1. Adventure and adventurers—Fiction. 2. Models (Persons)—Fiction.
3. Shoes—Fiction. 4. Orphans—Fiction. 5. Christian life—Fiction. 6. Kenya—
Fiction. I. Title.
PZ7.O81165Ris 2015
[Fic]—dc23
    2014016531

Editor: Mary Hassinger
Art direction: Deborah Washburn
Cover design and interior decoration: Jennifer Zivoin
Interior design: Ben Fetterley and Greg Johnson
Interior composition: Greg Johnson/Textbook Perfect

Printed in the United States of America

14 15 16 17 18 19 20 21 /QG/ 20 19 18 17 16 15 14 13 12 11 10 9 8 7 6 5 4 3 2 1

To my parents, Chuck and Carmella—
If I had one wish for all the Faithgirlz of the world,
it would be that they would have a mom and a dad
who are as loving, as generous, as encouraging, and as
faith filled as you two are.

"For shoes, put on the peace that
comes from the Good News
so that you will be fully prepared."

EPHESIANS 6:15 NLT

Chapter 1

Dear Sean,

How are you? I'm writing to say hi, and to tell you that you don't have to save me a donut at church this week. I'm flying to Kenya! I know, it sounds crazy, but my whole life's crazy now. Remember the shoe deal I got involved with? Well, that turned out to be a disaster. Yeah, the shoes are great and all, but the people who own the company aren't really who they say they are, and they're running from bad guys who want to kill them. Remember my goofy photographer, Flip? Well, he nearly fell off Half Dome! Then, right after I almost got eaten by a bear, I experienced my very first whitewater rafting trip — without a raft. Thankfully nobody's dead, but we're all pretty scraped up. I even have a broken hand, which is why my writing's so terrible.

Anyway, I heard you have a new friend named Morgan. I hope you don't "like" her like you "like" me. I know I've been saying since kindergarten that I'd never marry you, but lately I've been thinking it could happen ... someday. Riley O'Reilly might be a cool name to have after all ...

Whatcha writing, kiddo?" Flip's voice right next to my ear made me jump about a mile out of my seat on the jet.

"Nothing." I wadded the paper in my good fist. "How long have you been standing there looking over my shoulder?"

Flip shrugged. "I wasn't. Why'd you crumple it up?"

"Bad penmanship." I held up the glowing orange cast and examined the puffy fingers on my right hand. "I wish I broke the other hand instead. No ... wait. I wish *neither* of my hands were broken."

"You can use my laptop if you want."

"Thanks, but I wasn't going to send it anyway."

Flip raised an eyebrow. "So, it's a letter? I thought all you kids did was text these days."

"Well, in order to text, I would need a phone, and you guys took mine, remember?"

"But that was so you wouldn't accidentally divulge our secret location. You're kind of a chatty kid, you know."

"Yeah, but the bad guys found us anyway."

Flip scratched his head and thought a minute. "Okay, you have a point, there." Then he pulled my phone out of his pocket. "Here. You can have it back."

"Really?" I grabbed the phone out of his hand and ran my fingers over the sparkly pink cover. I pushed the ON button and hummed along with the cheery start-up tune. Then I noticed Flip's familiar smirk. "Hey ... what's the catch?"

"Yours won't work outside the U.S."

"That figures."

"But, you *can* use the camera part to take cool pics of giraffes and lions. And you can write all the texts you want to your boyfriend without worrying about sending them."

For that, I punched Flip in the arm. "He's not my boyfriend. And I thought you said you weren't looking over my shoulder."

"Hey, I'm just messing with you! That's what I do, remember? And you usually mess back. What happened to the fun Riley Mae Hart?"

I held up my cast again and stuck out my lower lip. "This happened."

Flip's older sister, Fawn, who's also my personal assistant at Swiftriver, came walking down the aisle carrying what looked like five daily servings of fruits and vegetables.

"Is he bothering you?" She plunked a napkin full of carrots in my lap. "Never mind, of course he is." Then she turned to Flip. "Stop it."

"What?" Flip threw his hands up. "I'm being a nice guy. I gave her phone back."

"Even so, I want you to go away." Fawn grinned and brushed him away with her hand.

Flip hobbled off in his ankle cast. Then we heard him from the back of the jet. "You girls should be nicer to me. I fell off a mountain, you know."

Fawn rolled her eyes then sat down next to me. "Did you take your malaria medicine?"

I barely nodded. I didn't want to talk about malaria, because that would mean we were really going to Africa, where apparently there were mosquitoes that could kill you. I already had people who were trying to do that. No need to add bugs to the list.

Fawn leaned over closer. "Ooh, I like your phone cover. Can I see some of your pictures?"

"Sure. But they're mostly of my friends." I pointed to one that was taken at children's church.

"Who's the strawberry-blond cutie?" Fawn asked.

My face heated up a little. "Oh, that's Sean. He's had a crush on me forever. But ..."

"But what?"

"I think it's over now." I grabbed a carrot off my lap, snapped it in half, popped both pieces into my mouth, and chewed and chewed and chewed.

"I doubt that very much," Fawn said.

I sighed. "He's hanging out with some new girl."

"Oh. Well, I'm sure she's not as sweet and wonderful as you are."

"You think I'm sweet and wonderful?"

Fawn smiled. "And beautiful, and much more put together than I was at twelve."

I sat up a little straighter and smoothed my wrinkled T-shirt. "You know, I'm turning thirteen in a few weeks."

Fawn gasped and almost dropped some broccoli on the floor. "What? Is that in the contract? Are you allowed to become a teenager?" She smiled and tried to force-feed me a disgusting green stalk, but I pushed it away.

"Probably not. Hey, maybe Swiftriver will finally let me out of that contract. Why don't we just turn the jet around right now and go talk to Bob Hansen about it in Fresno?"

Chapter 1

"But then you would miss your surprise birthday safari." Fawn put her hand to her mouth, like she had let out some long-kept secret.

"Safari, huh?" I pictured myself feeding friendly giraffes and smiled. "That sounds interesting." Then I pictured myself and the giraffes being swarmed by mosquitoes.

"But isn't it a little dangerous?"

Fawn chuckled and patted me on the cast. "This whole adventure has been dangerous, Riley. But hey—at least there aren't any bears in Africa."

Chapter 2

The flight to Africa was LONG. Hours and hours and hours. First we had to fly to New Jersey, and then to Switzerland for more fuel. Then we still had something like ten hours left to go. Whoever wrote that song about it being a small world after all was wrong. But at least the boring flights were smooth. The last time I was in a Swiftriver private jet, we crash-landed. Tyler, our fearless pilot, guaranteed that wouldn't happen again. And this time, we were in the "back-up" jet, which had been checked, double-checked, and re-checked for safety.

"Need something to do? Here you go." Flip returned from the back of the jet and sat down in the seat across the aisle from me. He tossed over a thick mailing envelope.

I caught it, pulled out a stack of papers, and read the first one.

Dear Riley Mae,

I saw you in *Outdoor Teen Magazine*, and I'd like to know if you were scared when you climbed Half Dome. I'm afraid of heights, but I want to try it anyway. What do you think I should do? Please write back!

Jessica

The next one was a printed-out email.

Subject: Girls in sports

Dear Riley Mae,

I love sports, but my dad won't let me sign up for any. He says there's only enough money for my brothers to play. What should I do?

Sarah

"Flip, where did these come from?"

"Your adoring fans. Some came to the Swiftriver office, and some were forwarded from Nate at *Outdoor Teen Magazine*. He said they're thinking of starting a column where you answer questions that kids send in. Whaddya say?"

"I can't answer these questions." I shoved the papers back in the envelope and tried to give it to Flip. "Tell whoever that I can't do a column."

He pushed it back. "Okay, but you still have to answer the letters."

"Why?"

Flip smiled big. "Because they're your fans. You have tons of them, kiddo."

"But I don't know *what* to tell them! I can't even solve my own problems right now."

I guess I got a little loud, because I woke up Mom, who had been napping a few seats in front of me. "Riley, what on earth is going on?" She stood up, stretched, and yawned. Poor Mom. She hadn't been sleeping much during the last week with all the Swiftriver nonsense going on.

"Nothing," I said. I jumped up and stormed to the back of the plane, looking for a place to hide. The bathroom was it.

Lord, what is going on? Why are you letting this happen to me? I prayed to go home. Why did you say no?

I allowed myself to cry for a minute or two. But then I realized that tears were bouncing off my cast. Oops, not supposed to get that wet. Time to straighten up.

I glanced up at my blotchy face in the mirror. "You're a grumpy mess, Riley Mae Hart." I wiped my eyes with my sleeve.

"Oh well. Might as well make the most of it."

I pulled a pen out of my pocket and scribbled on a paper towel:

Dear Jessica,
Don't climb Half Dome. You'll just fall off.
Blessings, Riley

Dear Sarah,
Don't play sports. You'll end up in Africa.
With Love, Riley

I smirked. "See, terrible answers." I flushed them and then I wondered, where does that stuff go in a plane, anyway? There were so many things I didn't know. And that was only one of the million reasons why I couldn't write a column.

Mom tapped on the bathroom door. "Riley, are you okay, honey? You need to come out. We'll be landing soon."

Landing. Finally. Too bad it had to be in Nairobi. I wished I had paid more attention in geography class. I had already made a fool of myself by asking what country Kenya was in. Everyone sure got a laugh out of that. Turns out that Kenya *is* a country on the *continent* of Africa, which I sort of knew from a song I learned when I was four, but I didn't really understand what a continent was back then. After my silly question about where Kenya was, my genius little brother, Brady, had to show me up by drawing a map. On the plane, I showed it to our friend, Kiano.

"Where do you guys live?" I asked.

Kiano pointed to a place on Brady's map that said *high*. "Oh, good, I like mountains."

He just threw his head back and laughed. Somehow, I must have had *that* wrong too. I decided not to ask anymore dumb questions right then, because at least I knew one thing:

Africa is hot.

Chapter 3

"How come it's not hot out here?" I shivered and was frustrated that I had packed my hoodie in my suitcase. "Are you sure we're in Africa?"

Kiano laughed again as he guided his daughters, Faith, Grace, and Hope, from the bottom of the jet steps toward the terminal.

"You will be surprised about the weather where we live," twelve-year-old Faith said. Then she turned to her dad. "Are we going to see our elephants today?"

Now *that* sounded exciting! I had always imagined kids in Africa riding elephants.

"Yes," Kiano said. "I think that Miss Riley Mae would love to see them too."

Just as Kiano said that, he opened up the terminal door and we were greeted by a sign hanging from the ceiling that said:

Smile, You're in Kenya!

"Okay, I need a group picture." Flip pulled his camera out of his bag. "Everyone under the sign. Wow. Our first day in Africa!" We all bunched together and faced Flip. He clicked his camera a couple of times and then frowned at me. "Shoe girl, did you leave your smile back in the States?"

I flashed him a real big, cheesy one.

He clicked. "Oh, good. You had me a little nervous there."

"Can you take a picture of just the girls?" eight-year-old Grace asked. "We have the same shoes on. We can send it to Sunday."

Faith, Grace, Hope, and I were all wearing the flaming-orange, Riley Mae "Sole Fire" running shoes. The girls' ten-year-old brother, Sunday, wears Sole Fires too. All the time. He doesn't even care that they're for girls. I wished he could be here in the picture with us instead of in Montana with his mom, fighting leukemia. At least when we left, he was doing well, recovering from a bone marrow transplant. Otherwise, I think it would be torture for his father Kiano and his sisters to be so far away from him.

"So, do each of you have your own elephant?" I asked the girls.

Grace and Hope giggled as Faith set me straight. "Mr. Flip fostered one for each of us at the elephant orphanage. We go to see them whenever we are in Nairobi."

Hope's eyes got big. "Mine is called Muna. That is my name!"

"I thought your name was Hope," I said.

"The name Muna means hope," Faith said.

Hope jumped up and down and pointed to herself. "Just like me! And wait till you see Muna, Riley. Her is so cute!"

Faith waved a finger at Hope. "*She. She* is so cute."

Hope looked confused. "That is what I said!"

Faith shook her head. "She refuses to learn proper English."

"She does better than most four-year-olds," I said. "Especially considering that she also speaks, uh ... what do you guys speak, anyway?"

"Swahili, and our tribal language is Kalenjin."

I tapped my fingers on my chin. "How will I know which one's which?"

Faith looked up toward the ceiling, and then put her hands on her hips. "I do not know how to help you with that. I am so sorry."

"Well then, Hakuna Matata!"

Faith's mouth dropped open. "What? It appears that you *have* learned some Swahili."

"No, I just watch Disney movies. You know, *The Lion King?* Hakuna Matata?" I shuffled my feet and shook my head back and forth, which made Grace and Hope laugh and dance around too. A few people in the terminal laughed at us.

"Jambo, Kiano!" A huge, dark man ran over to our group and wrapped Kiano up in a big hug. I had thought Kiano was big until then.

The girls laughed and squealed some more as they joined in the hug. Tears streamed down Kiano's face. A bunch of words that I didn't understand flew out of the mouths of the happy little group.

"You guys know each other?" No one answered, and I suddenly noticed that Flip, Fawn, and Mom were gone.

Strange. So I just stood there, near the hugging group, looking around. A chill ran through my body, so I crossed my arms over my chest and hugged myself. This was so awkward. And lonely. I looked back up at the sign:

Smile, You're in Kenya!

Was Kenya supposed to be a happy place? I tried to smile, but something felt fake. Yep. Cheesy. Hmmm. Maybe Flip was right about me leaving my smile in the States.

Chapter 4

Mom came back in a few minutes with Flip and Fawn. She waved some papers in the air. "Got the visas—wow, that was quicker than I thought it would be."

"Why do you need a credit card when you have Flip and Fawn? They've got tons of money." I turned to Flip. "I hear you're sponsoring elephants now too."

"These visas are actually permits to stay in the country," Fawn said. "Not credit cards."

"But," Flip added, "you'll be begging me for your own elephant once you see how cute they are."

He was right. The elephant orphanage was the most amazing place I had ever been.

"That is Muna! Her is getting big!" Hope pointed out the window at the smallest elephant as a volunteer held an extra-large bottle up to her mouth during the "kindergarten" feeding time.

"I don't get why there are so many elephant orphans." I scrolled through the collection of pictures at the information kiosk in the lobby. It even included some baby rhinos. "What happened to their parents?"

"Most elephants are killed by poachers who want their ivory tusks, or in the case of the rhinos, their horns."

Faith frowned. She scrolled farther on the kiosk to show me some gruesome pictures of animals that had been killed and had their faces chopped off.

"Ugh! Why would anyone do such a horrible thing?"

"Greed." Faith scrolled some more and found Grace's elephant, Matunga. "They discovered Matunga wandering all by herself near Lake Matunga."

"I'm writing a storybook about Matunga and how she finds her family someday," Grace said.

Faith pointed to another elephant on the screen. "This is my elephant, Chemi Chemi."

"They're so adorable! Can we touch them?" I *really* wanted to touch a baby elephant.

"Yes, follow me." Faith led us out of the lobby and pointed to a roped-off area that held the baby elephants. "We can go up and pet them if they come near."

I was at the rope in seconds. "They're not coming over."

"Give them time to eat first," one of the workers said. "They may be small, but they are still elephants, so they need lots of food."

No kidding. Each elephant was slurping through several big bottles.

"Where are the rhinos?" I asked.

"In cages," Faith said. "They are not as friendly as the elephants."

"Muna is all done!" Hope pointed as we watched the volunteer finish feeding the cute little elephant. But then Muna turned away from us and ran.

"Her is running away! Muna!" Hope ducked under the rope and ran after Muna.

"Hope! Come back right now." Faith reached her arms out, but didn't move.

"Oh no! What should we do?" Grace jumped up and down while holding the rope.

The adults were all gathered in a cluster talking to one of the orphanage workers. Other workers were still feeding their assigned elephants and didn't notice Hope on their side of the rope.

"I'll go get her." In seconds I was under the rope and behind some bushes, searching for Hope. I couldn't see her anywhere. I did see a bunch of friendly little elephants, though.

"Hey, have you guys seen a little girl?" The elephants just smiled back. I guess that's what they always do. Probably 'cause they're in Kenya.

Then I heard Hope's voice in the distance. "Muna, Muna!"

I ran toward the voice, up a little hill, and then down again toward a creek. There was Hope with Muna. Hope was covered with red dust, and she was laughing.

Muna was picking up the dust with her trunk and flinging it all over herself. Hope was getting the overflow.

I chuckled and jogged down closer. "Hope! You aren't supposed to go past the rope."

"But I had to see Muna. Her is my elephant."

I grabbed Hope's hand. Then Muna tossed me some dirt too—right in my face. It took a minute to spit it out of my mouth. "We need to hurry back."

"But, it is fun!" Hope said.

"We're not allowed to be here. It could be dangerous."

"I am not afraid, Riley."

"I know, but we hafta go." I tightened my grip on Hope's hand, and turned to walk back up the hill.

That's when we met up with the rhinoceros.

Chapter 5

He was trotting down the hill, right toward us. He wasn't huge—just a baby—but he wasn't smiling like the cute little elephants were.

"Uh-oh. Hope, don't move."

"Hello, Mr. Rhino," Hope said.

"Shh. We need to run, uh … that way. Or maybe that way." I tried to figure out the best way to go. But, which way was safest? I mean, did this little guy break out of his cage and bring a bunch of his friends with him? And were there lions anywhere around here? The rhino snorted and gained speed. That was it, I was going left.

"C'mon!" I pulled on Hope's hand, but she broke away from me and ran—straight toward Mr. Rhino. I reached out to grab her, but she was too fast, and I fell in a heap to the ground.

"AAAAAHHHHHHHHH!" Hope waved her hands and did a crazy dance just feet away from the rhinoceros. The rhino stopped and stared at her. I closed my eyes. *Help, Lord!*

"AAAAAAHHHHHHHHH!" Hope yelled again. Probably her last words.

Then she started laughing, and I figured she couldn't do that if she had been crushed to pieces, so I opened my eyes. She ran back to where I was sitting in the dirt. "That was so funny! He runned away."

A grown-up hand grabbed me by the elbows and lifted me back onto my feet. "Children should not be behind the rope." A serious-looking young man led Hope and me back to the visitor's area.

"My name is Kiptoo." He took us to an outdoor work sink and gave us some wet towels to wipe the red dirt off our faces.

"I'm sorry," I told Kiptoo. "She ran after the elephant, and I was trying to protect her."

Kiptoo laughed. "It appeared that she was protecting you."

"Yeah, well I was sort of shocked to see that rhino."

Kiptoo shook his head. "That was Rafiki. He keeps finding a way out of his cage. Thankfully, he is not as grumpy as the rest of the rhinos."

"I tried to grab Hope and run, but she got away from me."

Kiptoo wagged a finger. "You must never run. Food runs. You do not want to be food. Remember that."

"Even from lions?"

Kiptoo grinned. "Especially from lions. Not even Kenyans are fast enough to outrun a lion. Thankfully, there are no lions here at the orphanage."

"Okay, but if I come face-to-face with a lion somewhere else in Africa, am I supposed to run at it and freak out?"

Kiptoo frowned and crossed his arms. "No."

"Then, what?"

"Do not come face-to-face with a lion. That is what."

Something big came up behind me. I saw the shadow. Kiptoo's eyes focused on something behind my head, and then he ran off, so I figured it wasn't a lion. I turned around and looked way up and into the eyes of that big guy from the group hug at the airport.

"Jambo?" I said.

"Jambo." He smiled, but only for a second. "My name is Jomo. I will be watching you." He pointed toward the elephants.

"Oh. I'm so sorry. I was saving Hope ... or something like that."

"You were in no danger." He pointed to his eye. "I was watching."

"I'm really not a troublemaker." I reached up with my towel to wipe more dirt off my face. "Sometimes I accidently get into trouble, but don't worry, I heard what Kiptoo said about running and all ..."

The big man knelt down to my eye level and he put his finger to his lips. I shushed.

"You are no trouble." He pointed to his eye again. "I will watch for the mzungu." Then he pointed to the orange cast on my hand. "He will not hurt you again."

Then he stood up and covered me with his shadow. I tipped my head back to look at him and grinned.

"Okay, thanks," I said.

He turned and walked away, but only a few steps. Then he turned back around, crossed his arms, smiled, and pointed to his eye again.

Faith and Grace came around the corner and looked relieved to find us.

"I want to see Muna again," Hope said.

"Only if you promise to stay with me this time." Faith grabbed Hope's arm and didn't let go as we walked back to the roped-off area.

"Faith," I whispered. "Who is that?" I gestured to the big guy who was still watching my every move.

She whispered back. "That is uncle Jomo. He will keep us safe."

Whew. "What's a mzungu?"

"White man. Uncle Jomo will keep the bad ones out of our village."

Chapter 6

Dear Rusty,

Jambo! That means hi in Swahili. It's the only word
I know so far. Well, there's another word: mzungu,
which I found out means white man, or aimless
wanderer. I guess I'm considered a mzungu here in
Kenya. Yesterday, I wandered aimlessly—right into a
rhinoceros. Thankfully, I had four-year-old Hope to
save me. Boy, did I feel dumb.

But you should have seen the cute baby elephants!
They live here in Nairobi, at this elephant orphanage.
Most of their parents have been killed for their tusks,
which I think is disgusting. The poachers don't even
care if the baby elephants die without their mothers.
That reminds me, how's it going with your mom? I've
been praying that your dad will forgive her for leaving,
and that you will all be able to be a family again. I know
that would probably be a miracle, but hey, we found
your mom, and that was a miracle, wasn't it?
I miss you, TJ, and Sean (but don't tell him I said
that). I will probably be home as soon as I get this
photo shoot done for the running shoes. But here's
something funny: a guy named Kiptoo told me never to

run. Only food runs. I'm gonna tell Flip and Fawn about that. Then maybe I can come home sooner!

Love, Riley

P.S. Sorry for the sloppy writing. The cast is still on.

I think we should bring Jomo home with us," I said to Mom as we rolled our suitcases out of the hotel lobby and into the parking lot. "I bet he could talk Eric and Drew into leaving us all alone." I put fingers up to both of my eyes and then pointed them at Mom. "I will watch you," I said, and I grinned over at Jomo, who of course was off in the distance watching me.

Mom handed our suitcases one by one up to Kiano, who grunted as he lifted mine into the back of a trailer that was hitched to the back of one of our Jeeps.

"Too many shoes," Mom said, shaking her head. Then she turned to me. "I don't want you even thinking about Eric and Drew, okay? We've got people looking for them, and soon we'll know what part they played in all the Swiftriver accidents. Your job is to model shoes and enjoy our little African vacation."

"Are we gonna be home before school starts?"

She shrugged. "I'm not sure. Consider yourself home-schooled for now."

Grace had wheeled her Disney princess suitcase over to the trailer. "I have an idea. Riley could come to school with us."

Faith rolled her suitcase up and shook her head. "It is too far for her to run."

"You run to school? I thought only food runs."

Faith didn't smile at my joke. "We must run to school so we will arrive on time. Five kilometers each way, two times a day."

"What about the lions?"

"We watch out for them."

"You're kidding, right?" Never mind. Faith doesn't kid. So I changed the subject.

"How long is a kilometer again?" The only thing I'm worse at than geography is math.

"That can be your first homeschool assignment," Mom said. "Figure it out. I want the answer by the time we arrive in Iten."

Fawn brought her luggage next and left it for Kiano to load. She walked around to the right side of the Jeep, jumped in, and adjusted her seat to drive. It was weird seeing the steering wheel on that side of the vehicle! I guess this was how it worked halfway around the world from where I lived.

"Fawn, how far to Iten?"

Flip climbed into the passenger seat next to Fawn, spread out a map of Kenya, and put his index finger on Nairobi. Then he put his thumb on Iten and held up his hand with the space still in between. "About that far."

"Very funny," I said. "So how long does it take to get there?"

He spread his arms as wide apart as he could get them. "About that long."

"Ugh! Why didn't we just fly there?"

Flip put his hand to his heart. "And miss the adorable little elephants? And the bumpy Jeep ride?"

"What bumpy Jeep ride?"

"Get in, Shoe girl." Flip pointed to the open door of the next Jeep, where Mom was standing. "Unless, of course, you want to run."

"It would be good training for her for when we get to Iten," Fawn said.

"I still don't understand what the big deal is about running."

Jomo came up behind me and laughed, which made me jump. "In Iten," Jomo pointed to my eye, "you will see."

Chapter 7

I guess Kenya doesn't have a seat belt law. Or even a "sit in your seat" law. Good thing, because it was hard to actually stay in my seat with all the bumping. Our Jeep was the most crowded, with Jomo driving, Mom in front, and me, Faith, and Grace in the backseat. Hope rode with her dad in the other Jeep along with Flip and Fawn.

I was excited to leave Nairobi. Something about being in the crowded city the last couple of days had made me nervous. Even though Jomo was watching me, I still jumped every time I saw a curly blond head like Eric's bobbing around in the street. Last time I had actually seen Eric, he was supposed to have been one of the good guys. But after the accident on the river, and Eric's disappearance, everyone else was convinced otherwise. I still wasn't sure, but I had a broken hand to remind me to be extra careful.

"Riley, quit hogging the view. The other girls might want to see out too." Mom's always worried about being fair, but Faith and Grace had been to Nairobi National Park before. I had never seen any place like this. Ever. So I just stood in the middle of the backseat with my head poking out the open top of the Jeep. I took a whole bunch of blurry pictures with my phone since the Jeep never stopped bumping.

The trailer that was being pulled behind Flip and Fawn's Jeep made a horrible racket.

"What's in that thing, anyway?" I asked, since I knew none of us had brought that much luggage.

"You'll see," Mom said.

Just then, I spotted big shadows to the right. Bigger than Jomo shadows.

"Giraffes! Wow, look at them run! You'll never see that at the Fresno zoo!" I tried to take a picture with the Nairobi skyscrapers in the distance, but with the bumping it was no use. "Can we stop for a minute?"

Jomo pulled the Jeep over. Unfortunately, the giraffes went the other direction, so I missed the shot.

"Rats!" I slumped back down in my seat.

"Do not give up so quickly," Faith said. "This is Kenya." Then she pointed out the window. I watched, amazed, as a few zebras trotted by.

"Great, I didn't get them either."

Grace giggled. "You will see more and more and more. Do not worry."

Flip jumped out of his Jeep and hobbled toward us with his camera. "Woo-hoo! I got some great shots of those beauties! Did you see them, Riley?"

"Yeah. They were awesome! But you'll have to share your pictures. I missed them."

"What? You mean your sparkly phone didn't work so well?"

I bounced my phone up and down in Jeep-like fashion

and snapped a picture of Flip. I held it up for him to see. "I can't tell. Is this you or a zebra?"

Flip laughed. "Okay, I get it."

It was so weird watching wild animals roam free like that with the city so close. At home, I barely even see a dog running without a leash attached.

Flip pointed his big camera lens toward the ground at the back of our Jeep. "What's that wiggling over there?"

Jomo jumped out of the driver's side to look. Then, somehow, Flip ended up shoved in the backseat with me and the girls, and Jomo squealed the tires and took off down the road.

"Snake chase!" Grace yelled, and we all turned to look out the back, only to see what I guess was a snake, still in the distance, under the cloud of dust from our Jeep.

Faith crossed her arms and shook her head. "Grace likes to make up fantastic stories. Snakes do not chase cars."

"Oh, yes they do," Grace said. "My friend said that a snake crawled up into her bus once and took a ride on her suitcase."

"That is different than chasing," Faith said.

Either way, the whole thing gave me the shivers because I hate snakes. "Why didn't we just shove the Jeep in reverse and run it over?"

"For what purpose?" Faith said.

"I don't know. 'Cause it's a yucky snake?"

"I like snakes," Faith said. "But you have to be careful with the poisonous ones."

"Was that one poisonous?"

"Why do you think I'm shoved in here with you?" Flip said. The Jeep bumped and threw him sideways into me. Unfortunately, at that second, he was blowing a bubble with his gum and it stuck on my arm.

"Wow." Flip pulled a little gum off his upper lip. "Bad timing on that bubble. Sorry."

I pretended to gag and pulled some of the gooey stuff off my arm. I gave the sticky mess to Flip, who popped it back in his mouth.

"That is super gross, Flip."

Grace giggled.

"Can we get him out of here now?" I asked.

"Aw, c'mon, let me stay in the fun Jeep."

Jomo pulled over again, and Fawn pulled up next to us. "It's been so peaceful in here. Can you send a girl over instead?"

"We'll go," Faith said. She and Grace gathered up their backpacks and they both jumped in the front with Fawn. Fawn revved the Jeep, winked in my direction, and took off.

"I don't think Faith likes me," I said.

"Why not?" Mom asked.

"She doesn't *get* me or something. She doesn't laugh at any of my jokes."

"It's because they're bad," Flip put his index finger in his mouth as if he were choking himself.

"Grace laughs."

"Grace laughs at Faith not laughing."

"I don't think it's that she doesn't like you," Mom said. "I think she just has a very different life than you have. You should take this time to try to get to know her better."

"Faith is a very good girl," Jomo said. "Responsible."

"Sounds like we could all learn something valuable from Faith." Flip grinned in my direction and blew another bubble. I popped it with my finger and gum stuck all over his face.

Chapter 8

"So, Flip," Mom twisted her head around to face the backseat, "any news about how Sunday's doing?"

Flip's grin disappeared. "Yes, I talked to his mom this morning. He has a little cold, and his numbers are low."

"Are Brady and Dad still with him?" I asked.

Mom answered, "Yes. But they're going back to Fresno in a couple of days."

"Is that safe? I still don't get why they didn't come to Africa with us. Wouldn't Eric and Drew be after them too?"

"It's not likely," Mom said. "Plus, they're staying at Grandma's, and I have the department keeping an eye on them."

My mom's the chief of police in Clovis, California, which comes in handy, especially when bad guys are after you.

"And," Flip said, "your dad has to get busy reworking the flip-flop campaign, and then there's the snowboarding boots—"

I held up my hand. "Wait. Why is he reworking the flip-flop campaign?"

"We thought the pictures we took were too boring."

"So you're saying I froze by a pool in February for nothing?"

"Well, not for nothing," Flip sighed. "The boredom of it all helped us decide that we needed to go to a tropical island instead."

"Oooh! I vote Hawaii, but *only* if I can bring friends."

"Oh, really? You're getting demanding now that you're almost a teenager. Which island would you like to go to?"

Aack. Geography again. "I don't know. I've never been there. How about we just go to the best one?"

"Which is?" Flip raised his eyebrows.

"Why are you asking me?"

"Okay, Riley," Mom said. "Next homeschool assignment is to find out about all the Hawaiian Islands."

Flip pulled a book out of his backpack. "Try using this." It was a pocket travel guide for the United States.

I eagerly flipped to the chapter on Hawaii. I read about the different islands, and all the fun things we could do there. I imagined my friends TJ and Rusty and me learning to surf and doing the hula.

That's when our Jeep hit a huge rut in the road and knocked the travel guide off my lap.

Bye-bye, Hawaii. Back to reality. I was in Africa.

Chapter 9

We arrived in Iten about four hours later. Some of us got a little carsick as we climbed uphill on the winding, bumpy dirt road—okay, it was just me. Mom let me sit up front for a little while, which kept me from hurling, and that gave me a little time to talk to Jomo. He never said anything though. Once in a while he would look over at me and open his mouth like he was going to say something, but then he would just grin and shake his head.

"Jomo, do you have trouble with English?"

Jomo shook his head. "You speak many words."

"Yes, but do you understand me?"

He laughed. "Words, yes. You … not yet."

That's when I heard it. Thunder. That didn't make sense. The sky was clear.

Then I *saw* it. But barely. And it wasn't exactly an "it." It was a "them." A huge group of people, all running, but they went by us so fast that I had to look again to see if they were on scooters or something.

"Afternoon training run," Jomo said.

"Wow. What are they training for?"

Jomo shrugged. "To be better runners."

"Was that the whole town?" I asked.

"Practically," Flip said.

Another "shorter" huge group of people ran past us.

"Children returning home from school," Jomo said.

"So what's their hurry? Cookies baking in the oven?"

Jomo shook his head. "No. But maybe chapati."

"Does it have chocolate in it? I'd run that fast for chocolate."

Jomo laughed. "Chapati is flat bread. It is delicious. But you could not run that fast, even for chocolate."

"Why not? I can get to first base pretty quick."

"Sorry to tell you this," Flip said, "but right now you are the *slowest* kid in this town."

"How can you say that? You don't know the kids in this town."

"But I know about the town."

"Flip is correct," Jomo said. Then he pointed to a hand-painted sign at the side of the road. "There is a junior race tomorrow. You should go watch."

I looked back over my shoulder to catch a glimpse of the kids who had run past the Jeep. They were gone.

"How long is the race? Maybe I should run. Swiftriver made me some good running shoes. Maybe I'd only be the *second* slowest kid in town."

Jomo laughed. "And you might pass out before finishing the race."

Why did no one in this Jeep believe in my running abilities? Mom had seen me run during softball games, but she didn't say anything to back me up during the whole conversation. She just sat there, studying a map.

"Jomo," she said. "How far is your village from Iten?"

"Across many farms, about 80 kilometers."

"In the middle of nowhere." Mom smiled and looked up from the map. "Sounds perfect."

I stared out at the scenery surrounding the town of Iten. It wasn't at all what I had expected to see anywhere in Africa. Kiano had explained that this part of Kenya is at a high elevation and receives lots of rain. But even though it was beautiful, with the green hills, lush trees, and red dirt roads, Iten seemed to be in the middle of nowhere.

As we drove, I spotted a few houses and some buildings that that looked like small stores or businesses of some kind, but that was about it. Jomo said he was taking us to a training center for Olympic runners, so I kept waiting to turn a corner and see some huge stadium with a track and some hotels.

Nope.

"Is *this* it?" I jumped out of the Jeep as soon as it stopped and stretched my tight muscles a little, all the while hoping Jomo had made a mistake and would ask us to hop back in. This couldn't be the training center! It was just a big piece of land with a little wire fence around it and a house or something off in the distance.

Fawn's Jeep stopped behind us, and Faith, Grace, and Hope piled out.

"It is so wonderful to be here again!" Grace smiled.

"Uh," I said. "Where exactly *are* we?"

Faith looked at me with wide eyes and pointed off in the distance. "This is the training center where my mother trained for the Olympics. Sometimes we would come to visit, and they would let us swim in the pool."

I turned and squinted out at the property again. Were we talking about the same place? All I saw were big green bushes and interesting red dirt. I squatted down, grabbed some in my fist, and let it sift out between my fingers.

Grace tapped my shoulder and pointed. "It is there, behind that building."

I stood and brushed the dirt off on my jeans. "Is it a kiddie pool?"

Hope laughed. "No, it is for people, not kitties! And it is very big."

"You will see," Faith said. "This training center is very popular. Each room has its own shower too. We girls are lucky to stay here for the next two nights."

"Only the girls?" I looked around for Flip, Kiano, and Jomo. They were unloading our luggage from the trailer.

"Jomo will stay out in the courtyard," Mom said.

"Yeah, he'll be *watching*, right?" I turned to Jomo. "When will you sleep?"

"Later," he said. "God will help with that. For now, I will keep you safe, Miss Riley Mae. Do not worry."

Flip limped over with my suitcase. "And don't worry about me and Kiano, either. We're sleeping outside."

"You're sleeping outside—really?" I scanned the horizon for wild animal shadows.

"I have a friend in town who rents out tents," Kiano said. "But they have a cement bottom and are fenced off from wildlife."

"Oh, so it's just like the Fresno zoo, except it's the

humans that are caged in? Cool." I punched Flip in the arm. "Make sure you take lots of pictures of the lions pawing at the fence."

"And you enjoy the pool with that cast." He punched back.

"Ugh, I hate this thing. Mom, when did you say we could saw it off?"

"A few more weeks. We'll go into the city and have a doctor switch it out for a removable one."

"I could take care of it with a hacksaw right now," Flip said. "I may have one in the trailer."

My hand felt hot and itchy, so I thought that sounded fabulous. "Yeah, let's do it. I can always wrap it up in a bandage or something afterward."

"No," Mom said.

Fawn shook her head. "You guys are crazy."

"I am hungry." Faith rubbed her belly. "And if I am going to race tomorrow, I would like to eat some ugali."

"Wait, you're going to race tomorrow?" I crossed my arms and turned to Flip. "See! Faith's racing so why can't I?"

"Faith is fast," Jomo said.

"And the sign said that they are offering prize money this time." Faith smiled and grabbed her backpack and suitcase.

All of us girls followed, dragging our stuff along. Jomo helped me with my extra suitcase of shoes since I couldn't grab it with my annoying cast.

I waved back to Flip and Kiano. "See you tomorrow! Hakuna Matata!"

I'm glad I wasn't sleeping in a human zoo.

Chapter 10

I was happy to discover that the training center was bigger than I first thought. In the front of the main building was the courtyard, which was surrounded by those beautiful green bushes. In one area the bushes opened up to let a little path through.

Hope pointed to the path. "That way to the pool," she said, and ran off, disappearing in seconds.

Faith dropped everything and went after her sister. She was back shortly, dragging a frowning Hope.

"Let go of me. I want to swim!"

"First," Faith said, "we must find Miss Lorie. She will want to greet us and show us to our rooms."

Hope wiggled and squirmed until Fawn took her by the hand. "You're not even wearing a swimsuit, Hope. Why don't we unpack, and then I'll bring you to the pool."

"Okay, but can we hurry? I love swimming!" Hope tried to drag Fawn along, pulling her by the hand.

Fawn turned to Faith. "You don't have to worry about your little sisters tonight. I'll take care of them. You just find food and get some rest for the race tomorrow."

We were almost to the front door when a tall, slender African woman wearing what looked like an Olympic warm-up suit came out to greet us.

She smiled and held her hand out to me. "I am Lorie Kipjabe. Welcome to my training center! You must be Riley Mae."

I thought this lady was brilliant for picking me out of the crowd, until I realized that I was the only white-skinned young girl in the group.

"Yeah, that's me," I said.

"Did you have a pleasant trip?"

"It was good, but bumpy."

Lorie crossed her arms and looked concerned. "I am sorry about that. It can be that way in Kenya sometimes. But I am glad you have made it here safely." She patted me on the shoulder. "We will take good care of you. And did I hear that you will be modeling for some photos for an advertising campaign?"

"Yes, for these Sole Fire running shoes." I pointed to my feet. "But everyone tells me that I won't be able to run here or I'll faint or something. What do you think?"

Lorie laughed. "The elevation of Iten is eight thousand feet. The air is thinner. That is why athletes from around the world come, so they can get used to it. You are a young athlete, so I think you could be trained quickly."

"I knew it!" I stomped my foot. "Wait till I tell Flip."

Lorie then turned to give Faith a hug.

"It is amazing that *you* are here right now, Faith. Did you see that there is a junior race tomorrow? First prize is 1000 shillings."

"I can hardly believe that! You have never given out prize money before."

"Well, I thought it might be fun to see how much faster you all can run for it."

Lorie opened the door leading into a rather plain lobby. It had a few brown couches pushed against the walls and a small desk in the corner. Lorie reached into a desk drawer and pulled out keys.

"I have two rooms available for the six of you. I am sorry I do not have more space. But each room has its own bathroom and three beds."

Fawn took one of the keys. "That will be fine. We really appreciate the accommodations on such short notice." Then she turned to Grace and Hope. "Would you two girls like to room with me? We can stay up late and play games."

"Yes!" The girls followed Fawn, leaving me, Mom, and Faith in the lobby with Lorie.

Faith shook her head. "I should have gone to take care of them. They are a lot of work sometimes."

Mom patted Faith on the arm. "They'll be fine. We need to get you some food and some sleep, remember?"

Lorie grinned. "Here, let me help you take your luggage to your room. After you are settled, you can meet me in the kitchen for some ugali."

"Ew, what?" I wasn't so sure that food starting with the "ew" sound would be any good.

Faith rubbed her belly. "That sounds delicious!"

Okay then. With a reaction like that, I figured ugali had to be as delicious as the best-tasting chocolate in the world.

Chapter 11

Turns out ugali is a big, white blob. Of what, I had no clue.

I watched as Faith grabbed a ball of it with her hands and worked it like Play-Doh until it was the shape of a spoon. Then she filled the spoon with something that looked like mushy spinach, and she took a big bite.

"Mmm. That is so good!" She wiped her mouth with a napkin. "You should try some, Riley."

I pushed my finger into the big blobby stuff. It looked harmless enough, and since Faith wasn't gagging, I decided to chance it. I shaped a spoon too, and scooped up some of the veggie goop. I took a bite, chewed a minute, and prayed I wouldn't have to spit it out with everyone watching. The white stuff tasted a little like the homemade Play-Doh Mom used to make—kind of plain, a little salty. (Yes, once I actually took a bite of the Play-Doh. Not the best idea.) The veggies were definitely not my favorite, but then, vegetables *never* are.

Faith gobbled up several spoons before I managed to get my first one down.

"This is . . . interesting," I said.

Lorie looked at me and tilted her head. "Would you like something else?"

I put down my half-eaten glop and wiped my fingers with a napkin. "What else do you have?"

"No," Mom said, and gave me a funny look. "This will be fine for all of us. Thank you for preparing it."

Faith was still gobbling away. "I feel stronger already," she said.

Mom grabbed a big chunk of the ugali and shaped it into a monster-sized spoon. She packed it full of veggies and placed it in front of me. "Here you go," she said. "This will give you energy for the photo shoot tomorrow. You might be doing a little bit of running too."

I swallowed hard. "Do I have to?"

"It will help, Riley," Faith said. "All the good runners eat ugali."

"Well, Flip told me that I was a terrible runner, so I guess I can pass on eating it."

Mom shook her head. "He didn't say terrible, he just said you'd be the slowest in this town."

Lorie chuckled. "Your friend Flip is correct."

I frowned at that.

"But do not be discouraged. These children have been running their whole lives. You will be amazed when you see the race tomorrow. And we can teach you some techniques that will help you improve your speed."

Mom pointed at my plate. "But first, you need to eat."

And so I did. It tasted worse the more bites I took. But if Faith was right, that all the good runners ate ugali, maybe if I choked down a little more I might have a chance to be faster than at least one of the kids tomorrow—if I could just figure out how to sneak into that race!

Chapter 12

I woke up early the next morning, before Faith and Mom. My stomach was growling like a bear. Obviously ugali doesn't carry you through the night like, say, pizza does. I had to go find a snack. I somehow dug my clothes out of my suitcase and snuck out of the room without Mom's or Faith's eyes cracking open. Then I realized I should have left a note for Mom, so I made my way down the hallway toward the lobby so I could look for a piece of paper and a pen. I expected the place to be empty, but I was surprised to see lots of sweaty African women in athletic clothes sprawled out on the couches talking with one another. When they saw me, they popped up on their feet, and I ended up standing inside a circle of a few of them.

"Hello," the one with the red shirt said.

"Uh, hi." I looked around. The ladies were all staring at my feet.

"I like your shoes," said the tallest one with the big smile.

I felt my face heat up and I wondered if it glowed as brightly as my orange Sole Fires.

"Thanks. I like yours too."

They all laughed. The same woman spoke again.

"Really?" Then she bent down and took both of her shoes off and held them out to me. "I hate them. You may have them."

The group laughed louder. My face got hotter. Then the woman smiled and put the shoes down on the floor. "I am teasing you. I had a terrible run today. You should keep your bright shoes instead." Then she introduced herself. "I am Natalie." She reached out to shake my hand, and I had to offer the left one because of the cast.

"Oh," one of the women said, "your cast matches your shoes. How stylish!"

Natalie introduced the other women in the circle, but the only name I could remember was Mary because there were two of them.

I smiled. "I'm Riley Mae—"

The Mary with the short hair interrupted, "Yes! We know who you are. You are so cute." The women laughed again, and I reached up to smooth my bed hair down. I hadn't even looked in a mirror yet, which is never a good idea when it comes to my hair.

I tried to change the subject, "So, have you already been out running today?"

"Yes," Natalie said. "Our first training run of the day."

"How far did you go?"

"Twenty kilometers or so."

That seemed far, and I did the math later to find out it was twelve miles.

"Wow. You must be tired."

"Not so much," Natalie said. "Just frustrated that I came in last."

"I know what you mean. My photographer told me that I would be the slowest-running kid in this town."

"That may not be true," the Mary with the long braids said. "You should race today and find out."

Finally, someone who understood my frustration! "See, that's what I think. But I doubt I'll get a chance. The people I came with say I'll faint."

"It could happen," Natalie said, "if you are not trained. But you are an athlete, correct? That is why you are the outdoor shoe model?"

"Yeah."

"You should be fine then."

I wished Flip could have been in on this conversation.

"So, how long is the race today?"

Natalie rubbed her chin and thought for a moment. "For your age, there are two distances. One is 1.5 kilometers and the other is 3.5 kilometers."

I gave her a blank stare.

She smiled. "Approximately one mile and two miles."

I choked on my own spit. "I've never run two miles in my life. At least not altogether, at the same time."

"That could be a problem," short-haired Mary said.

"Maybe I can do the one-mile race," I said. "Our softball coach makes us run almost that much after practice."

Natalie nodded. "I think you can do it."

I crossed my arms and smiled. "Thank you. It's nice to have someone believe in me. Hey, do you ladies have any idea how I might be able to sneak into the short race? I have a little something to prove to my doubters."

"I do not know about that," the red-shirted lady said. "I think you should ask your parents nicely for permission."

Short-haired Mary shook her head. "That will never work. I remember asking my parents nicely if I could become a runner, and they said no."

"So, how did you get here?" I asked.

"One day I told them I was leaving the village, and I ran here. Miss Lorie felt sorry for me, so she helped me out until I won some races and earned some money."

"Well," I said, "that's a little more serious than my situation."

"It does not matter," long-braids Mary said. "All of us have had someone tell us we should not be running for some reason. I think we should stick together. Natalie, we can help Miss Riley Mae get into that race, right?"

Natalie thought for a moment, and then put her hands on my shoulders. "Okay. But only if you are sure that you will not be in trouble with your family."

I shrugged. "It will be fine with them, I'm sure. I just want it to be a surprise."

She smiled. "Then I think we are the perfect people to help you."

It turned out that these ladies were assisting Lorie with registering all the kids for the different races. Natalie told me she would register me for the one-mile race under the name Mae "Kiplabat," which, in Kalenjin, means I was born when someone was running. Well, in this case, they said it could mean that I showed up when they were finished running. Close enough, and the name sounded cool, so I agreed.

"Now, I have to figure out how to sneak up to the starting line without anyone noticing me."

"That is impossible," short-haired Mary said. "Your white legs will be a giveaway."

"But what if she wore running tights?" Natalie ran down the hall, into a room, and came back with a green windbreaker. "And you can use this to cover your arms and keep the hood over your head until the gun goes off. Pinch it in front of your face and pretend to shiver. People will think you are trying to stay warm."

Long-braids Mary looked confused. "But it is not cold outside."

I put on the windbreaker and pinched the hood to cover my face. Then I held out my left hand to Natalie. "My name is Mae Kiplabat. I am a fast runner. Nice to meet you."

Natalie shook my hand. "I think this might work." Then she looked down at my feet. "But are you going to wear those shoes? They might attract attention."

I had forgotten about the Sole Fires. "Yeah, they kind of glow, huh?"

"Better to wear mine," Natalie said.

"No!" Long-braids Mary took off her shoes, smiled real big, and handed them to me. "Hers are too slow. Mine work better."

The ladies all laughed. I tried on the shoes. They fit perfectly.

"What is going on in here? A morning party?" Lorie Kipjabe entered the lobby with a platter of bananas. "I hope this means that you are all ready for our busy day. The children will be arriving in two hours."

"Yes," Natalie said. "We are ready. I have assigned all the women jobs, and we will set up the tables soon."

Lorie smiled and handed me a banana. "I am surprised to see you up so early, after your long journey yesterday." Then she scrunched her eyebrows together and pointed to Mary's shoes that were on my feet. "Were you out training with these ladies?"

I shook my head. "No, just seeing if their shoes will make me faster." I jumped up and down and ran in place a little.

"The shoes have little to do with being fast," Lorie said. "You will see what I mean when the children arrive. Would you like to participate today, Riley?"

Wow. Maybe getting in one of the races would be easier than I thought.

"Sure!" I said.

Lorie smiled. "I love your enthusiasm. I will talk to your mother. Maybe you can help give out water at the end of the race."

"Oh, okay." Big let-down.

Lorie must have seen my disappointment. "Or maybe there is another job you would like to do?"

Natalie came to my rescue, "We will find a perfect job for her."

"All right, then," Lorie said. "I am off to the kitchen to see about breakfast for our guests. I will see you ladies out at the races."

The ladies all grinned and waved good-bye to Lorie. I followed her into the kitchen to eat some ugali—or hopefully something else that would give me super speed in less than two hours.

Chapter 13

Mom and Faith eventually woke up and came into the kitchen for some breakfast. All I was able to eat was one more banana, since now my stomach was a little nervous, knowing I was actually going to race against a bunch of fast Kenyan kids. I escaped out to the courtyard to get some air, and I practically ran into Jomo, who was standing alert next to the door.

"Habari zasubuhi, Riley Mae."

"Wow, that's a mouthful. What does it mean?"

Jomo smiled. "It means good morning."

"Oh. Well, habari za … za … uh. Good morning to you too. Did you get any sleep last night?" I don't know why I asked. I already knew the answer.

Jomo shook his head. "I enjoyed looking at the moon. Are you going somewhere?"

"Nope. Just coming out here. To, uh … stand. And maybe look around. I'm helping with the races today. Did you see some African women come by here a little while ago?"

Jomo nodded. "They went for a ride in a truck. To take tables to the field." He pointed up the road. "That is where the races will start."

"Oh." I shielded my eyes from the sun and looked that direction. "I think I was supposed to go with them."

"No, they said they will be back for you later."

"So . . . you talked to them?"

"Of course."

It occurred to me that it was going to be impossible to pull off my little "sneak in the race" trick unless I changed it up a bit. Jomo's job was to keep a close eye on me, so he would know exactly who was under that green windbreaker hood. And, who was I kidding? So would my mom. She's no slouch either, with her cop senses and everything.

Just then Flip and Kiano entered the courtyard. Kiano looked all bright and happy, but Flip looked like he had a fight with a pillow and lost.

"What happened to you?" I asked. I pointed to his head and covered my mouth as I giggled. "Your hair's messed up, and not in a fashionable way, if you know what I mean."

Flip smoothed his hair back with his hands and rubbed his eyes.

Kiano smiled. "It seems that Flip had some trouble sleeping in the tent listening to all the wildlife sounds."

"Oooh, what kinds of sounds?"

"Growling," Flip said. "And then there was ripping and chewing of carcasses sounds and fighting over meat kinds of sounds. And the screaming was deafening . . ."

"Screaming? Animals scream?"

"No. That was me," Flip said. "But thankfully I woke myself up and realized that some of the other sounds were just in my dreams. I think." He turned to Kiano. "Do we *have* to sleep in those tents again tonight?"

Kiano laughed. "I will see if Lorie knows of another place we can stay. Indoors."

"Yes," Flip said. "Let's go find her now. I need to find about a gallon of coffee too."

I pointed toward the door to the lobby. "I think you'll find both in the kitchen."

"Perfect," Flip said. "Riley, are you ready to look like a runner today for our photo shoot?"

"Don't you worry. I'm ready for this one." I held my cast up. "My feet aren't broken, remember?"

Flip stared at me carefully for a minute. "Well ... aren't *you* chipper this morning? I guess sleeping inside is the right choice in Africa."

"Yeah, I guess. And some of the women runners recruited me to help with the races. Isn't that cool? I want to be near the finish line to cheer Faith on. That won't mess up the photo shoot, will it?"

"No," Flip said. "We all want to be there to watch her run."

"She will win," Kiano said. "Just like her mother always did when she ran here. And then she can use the money to help with her high school tuition. God is good."

"I don't get that," I said. "Why does she have to pay for high school?"

"Because she would like to go to a national school," Kiano said. "In Nairobi."

"Nairobi? But that's so far away from your home."

"Yes. It is a boarding school. She will go there to live, and come home only once in a while. It is worth it for a quality education. But she also must get high marks on her tests to be accepted."

"That sounds stressful." No wonder Faith is so serious all the time.

Right then, the ladies in the old truck returned.

"Oh, hey guys," I said. "I gotta run. I think these women have an assignment for me. So ... well, I'm gonna go, okay? See ya!"

I took a couple of steps backward, with Flip still staring at me, rubbing his chin.

"O ... kay," he said. "See you later, at the race."

Natalie jumped out of the driver's side door. I ran over and stopped her before she could come within hearing distance of the guys. "Hey, we've got a problem."

Short-haired Mary joined our little huddle. "What is the matter? Are you sick?"

"Oh, no. I just think we need to change the plan. I kind of forgot that I have a bodyguard, not to mention a policewoman for a mom and a photographer who's in my face all the time. There's no way I'll be able to pull off that disguise without them knowing."

"Oh, dear," Natalie crossed her arms. "Maybe you should just ask them if you can race. We could help you persuade them."

"No. I have a better idea. And if you help me out, I think there's a way I can sneak into that race right under all their noses."

Chapter 14

The next two hours flew by. I thought we'd be doing a whole lot more setup for the races, but events in Kenya are a lot simpler than in Fresno. Basically, there was one table for each race, and each kid had to come up to the table and sign their name next to a number on a list. The ladies would then give them a handwritten number on a piece of paper to pin on their shirt. That was it. Then they just had to wait until their race was called and line up behind a row of small rocks on the oval dirt track.

Soon kids came walking in from all directions. Most of them were by themselves—no parents. They weren't wearing what I would call "athletic clothing," they just looked like they were dressed to play. All of them were smiling, and they seemed super excited to pin on their not-so-fancy race numbers.

Long-braids Mary came and handed me a number paper and a safety pin. "Mae Kiplabat," she whispered. "You will be running in the last race, and you are number thirteen. I hope you do not find it unlucky."

I grabbed the paper, folded it up, and put it in my pocket. "Of course not. I'm almost thirteen, so that's a good number. Plus, my family doesn't believe in luck—good or bad."

"Oh?" Mary looked like she wanted an explanation for that.

Okay, I thought, *I'll give it a try.*

"My family is Christian. We believe that God's in charge, and he'll be there to help us in good times or bad."

She smiled. "Well, I hope that the number thirteen brings you good times then."

I don't think she got it at all. I guess I needed to work a little on my explanation.

"Riley!" Mom waved me over to a dirt patch where she, Fawn, and the girls were sitting on a blanket. I checked to make sure my number was good and hidden in my pocket and ran over.

"Hey." Fawn pulled on the sleeve of my running shirt. "You sure dressed the part. Photo shoot's not till later."

"Yeah. But you know how Flip is always taking candids." I pointed over at a large group of children who were playing a hand-clapping game. "How come *they're* not dressed the part?"

"They wear what they have," Fawn said. Then she smiled. "They can run in anything."

"We have to run to school in our uniforms every day," Grace said.

"We saw kids running home from school the other day. It's July. Don't you guys get a summer break or something?"

"Next month we will be off for a little while," Grace

said. "When we return to our village, we will have three weeks of school before the break."

Hope's eyes brightened. "Do I get to go to school?"

"Not until you turn five," Grace said. Then she shook her head. "And then we will have to leave earlier in the morning since you are such a slowpoke."

Hope jumped up and ran in a circle around us. "I am not! I have been practicing to run fast like Faith. Look at me!"

We all clapped as Hope ran and stirred up the dirt around us.

Fawn coughed and waved the dirt from her face. "That is fast! But I think right now you should sit down and watch the start of the race, okay?"

Hope stopped running. She shaded her eyes with her hand and looked over toward the starting line. "Is this Faith's race?"

"Not yet," Grace said. "This is for the five- and six-year-olds. It is my favorite, because they just play and have fun. Sometimes they even forget to finish the race."

We watched as the starter held up the gun. The little kids covered their ears, and stood there shocked when they heard the bang. They laughed for a second, but then took off super fast, kind of like my brother Brady does when he grabs a warm cookie off the cooling rack even though my mom says not to.

I couldn't help but giggle, watching their little legs flailing around. One little girl fell down, and a bunch of other girls stopped to help her up and brush the dirt off her skirt. A little boy, who was leading the pack on the other side of the track, saw the girl and ran across the middle to go help her too.

"That must be her brother," Mom said.

Fawn smiled. "Flip did stuff like that for me when we were growing up."

I raised my eyebrows at Fawn. "So he's not one hundred percent goofball?"

"Well, he's one hundred percent *caring* goofball." Then she dropped her chin. "And he's pretty much all I have."

I almost asked *what about Eric?* But I caught that stupid remark before it tumbled out of my mouth. I love when that happens.

But I still wondered. Eric is Flip's and Fawn's half-brother, and they spent ten years living together in the same house before their parents divorced. That had to count for something! Besides, the possibility that Eric was trying to destroy his brother and sister's business just didn't make sense to me. Yet he was nowhere to be found after the accident in Montana when Drew pulled the volleyball net across the river, throwing our rafting guide, Matt, and then eventually me into the raging waters.

"See?" Grace pointed over to the kids helping the little girl who fell. "They have forgotten they are in a race." She grinned.

The kids were almost all walking by then, holding hands and giggling. They were fast all right, but most of them probably didn't really understand they weren't supposed to play with friends while racing. As they came across the finish line, the crowd clapped ... and so did the kids.

In the meantime, more little kids were lining up behind the rock starting line.

"Who are they?" I asked.

"Seven- to ten-year-olds," Grace said. "Then next will be the girls' and boys' junior races." These kids shot off the line as soon as the gun sounded and they didn't stop for anything. I wondered if I could have beaten any of them.

Kiano came up behind us and urged us to move closer to the track for Faith's race, which was next.

"Faith!" Kiano yelled over to his daughter, who was over by the rock starting line pinning on her number. She looked up and waved him over. Then Kiano turned to me. "Would you like to come pray with us, Riley?"

"Sure!" I jogged to catch up with Kiano, who had already started over to meet his daughter.

"Are you nervous?" I asked Faith as I reached out to grab her hand to pray.

"A little," she said. "I did not run much in Montana. But we will see how it goes. God knows I need the money."

Kiano grabbed both of our hands so that we were in a little circle, and he bowed his head, so I did too.

"Heavenly Father, please help Faith to do her very best, and to worship you as she goes. Amen."

Natalie yelled for the runners to take their marks. I tried to pat Faith on the back but I missed because she crouched down just as I reached out. When she came back up she handed me her Sole Fire running shoes. "Can you hold these for me?"

Out of the corner of my eye, I saw the line of runners forming at the rock start. Natalie held up the gun.

"Sure … but don't you need these? The race is starting!"

"I have to go," Faith said, and she ran over with the others. She reached the start just as the gun sounded. Then she took off, in her bare feet, and she made it to the front of the pack by the time the group rounded the first corner.

Everyone in the area seemed to stop what they were doing to watch this race. Flip had set up his camera equipment on a little hill overlooking the track and clicked pictures. Even the teeny kids were watching, clapping, and cheering.

"Go, Faith!" Grace and Hope jumped up and down as their sister passed on the first lap.

By the end of the second lap, three girls had established a large lead, and one of them was Faith. Then they left the track and took off down the dirt path through the bushes.

Kiano looked down at his watch. "They will return very soon."

I fixed my eyes on the path and prayed that Faith would be the first one I saw coming back. While they were gone, I thought about the growling and ripping and chewing of carcasses that Flip talked about, and I hoped that none of that was going on anywhere near where the girls were running.

"Does watching this make you want to be a runner, Riley?" Fawn had come up behind me, and her comment made me jump. I dropped Faith's shoes.

I reached down to pick them up. "How come she's not wearing these? Won't they help her run faster?"

"No," Kiano said. "Watch carefully when the runners come back. All the slowest ones are wearing shoes."

"It is what we are used to," Grace said.

"Without shoes," Fawn said, "you run more naturally on the balls of your feet, which makes your stride more efficient."

"Then how come we don't run barefoot in America?" I asked.

"It is *not* what you are used to," Grace said, and then she laughed. "And you have soft feet."

Soon the runners returned from the path. I squinted to try to see Faith. The first girl came in, but she had very short hair. Not Faith. Another girl followed. Not tall enough to be Faith.

Then I saw her. She was in third place, with her tight and long beaded braids flopping on the sides of her shoulders.

"Something happened," Kiano said. "She should not be in the third position."

Oh, no. What could have happened? I started praying for Faith to catch up.

"Go, Faith!" I yelled.

By the end of the third lap, she was just a few feet behind. As she rounded the curve where I was, we made eye contact, and all of a sudden, her serious frown turned upside down into the most gleaming smile I had ever seen. Her legs began to move faster, and the backs of her feet almost kicked her backside. The two girls in the lead looked like they were slowing down, but it wasn't that at all. Faith was running faster and faster with every step. The crowd started cheering wildly and yelling Faith's number.

"Thirty-three! Thirty-three!"

With only one curve left, Faith had caught up to the two girls. They turned their heads, and looked surprised to see Faith coming up from behind—right in the middle of them. I expected to see some elbow jabs, or something to keep Faith from passing. But instead, the girls moved over and made space for her to join them in a line of three. But that only lasted for a second. Faith kicked into an even faster gear and blew by them right toward the finish line.

Kiano was waiting with a huge hug as his daughter finished in first place! Lorie Kipjabe was there too, giving high fives to each junior girl who finished the race.

I rushed over to join the excitement. "Faith! That was amazing! How did you catch up so fast?"

"And a better question," Kiano said, "what happened to put you so far behind?"

"I crashed," Faith said, between heavy breaths. She pointed out toward the bushes. "The three of us were together most of the time, and I was near the edge of the path. I did not see the rock coming, so I tripped on it and went down on my face!"

That would explain the shrubbery in her hair and the dirt on her forehead.

"We better get you cleaned up." Fawn led Faith over to one of the tables where it looked like they had a first-aid kit.

"The boys are starting!" Hope pointed over to the rock starting line where Natalie shot the gun and a huge group of junior boys took off down the track. My stomach jumped when I remembered that my race would be next.

I needed to get over to Natalie to put our plan in action.

"Okay, guys," I said, "the ladies need me to help out in this next race. I'll be right back."

I jogged over to the side of the track by the rock start. A smiling Natalie met me there.

"Here's your weapon," she said, and she winked.

"Thanks." I put it in the same pocket as my secret number. "This is going to be fun."

Flip tripped a little walking down from where he was taking photos up on the hill. "Hey, Riley, what do you think? I told you these Kenyan kids are fast. I got some great pics of them zooming around."

"Yeah, they're fast all right."

Flip gave me a funny look, and limped over toward a group of kids who were lining up to get ready to run. He talked to them for a minute, and gave them something that they stuffed into their pockets. Whatever it was seemed to make them really happy. Fawn's right, Flip is a caring goofball.

Natalie yelled for the kids who were running in the "junior fun race" to come to the start line. When everyone was assembled, she addressed the crowd:

"I would like you all to meet a very special girl from the United States. Her name is Riley Mae, and she is here to learn more about running and to model shoes for an outdoor collection for girls. Please give her a nice welcome."

The crowd clapped, but I could barely hear because my heartbeat was pounding in my ears.

"Riley will be starting our race for us today."

Everyone looked surprised. Flip dragged himself up the hill and began clicking pictures.

Natalie looked at me. "Anytime you are ready, Riley."

I reached into my pocket and pulled out the cap gun — my weapon of distraction. I held it up in the air. My hand shook a little. "Ready runners! Take your mark ... get set ..."

I pulled the trigger, and the shot rang out. The kids took off.

And so did I.

Chapter 15

The first few steps of my run were awkward since I was trying to dig the paper out of my pocket. I pinned on number thirteen and then I pumped my arms and legs real hard—just like I do when I'm running to first base in a softball game.

For the first half-lap, I did great. The beautiful red and green colors of the African scenery blurred past me, and I felt like I was running on one of those conveyer belt things you find in airports. I was actually up with the first third of the pack! Then something weird happened. I was breathing hard, and air was going in and out of my lungs, but for some reason, I felt like I couldn't propel myself forward anymore. And soon, though I was huffing and puffing, I was having trouble getting air. I thought I'd have to quit—which would have been humiliating—but then I heard people cheering for me.

Flip was the loudest. "Go, Riley! Beat one kid!"

And then I saw Kiano, on the other side of the track. As I ran past him, his eyes met mine and I heard his loud, clear yell:

"Slow down your pace!"

But it sounded more like this:

"Slooooooowwww dooooooowwwwn yooooouuuur paaaaaaacccceee ..."

Slow down?

I dropped back from the first third of the group to the middle group and tried to catch my breath. No good. My breathing got heavier. So I dropped to the last third. Still no good. Thankfully, there were a few stragglers behind the last third, so I fell in with them. They smiled and waved at me as I slowed my pace and started to feel better.

One of them yelled, "Go, Mae Kiplabat!"

What? How did they know *that* name?

I suddenly realized that I didn't know what I was supposed to do at the end of the second lap. In all the other junior races, the runners had left the track and gone out to scary land. I remembered the lions, and I think a burst of fear caused me to run a little faster. I pulled ahead of the back-of-the-pack stragglers. I watched as the runners in front of me continued the third lap on the track. Whew. At least I wouldn't have to go out and possibly get eaten today.

With only one lap left, I heard more cheering from the crowd. The front group had finished the race. I passed by Fawn and the girls, who clapped and yelled. Even my mom was jumping up and down.

"Go, Mae Kiplabat!" she yelled.

Huh?

The last lap seemed like a mile in itself. My legs ached and my chest hurt as my lungs gasped for air. I began to hear feet pounding up from behind, and one by one, the stragglers caught up and passed me.

One girl who went by grabbed my hand. "Let me pull you," she said. So I let her drag me a few steps.

When she finally dropped my hand, she turned to look at me. "You are almost there, Mae!" Her face was covered with white dots. Or at least I thought it was, until another kid passed and there were white dots all over his shirt. I blinked hard a few times, and then a black outline appeared around everything I looked at. That outline got thicker and thicker and blocked more and more of the scenery, until all I saw at the finish line was Faith waving me across and holding out her hands.

Then I saw nothing.

* * *

"Riley! Riley!" I heard Faith's voice, so it must have been her pulling me up by the arms, but her face was blurry, so I wasn't sure.

My knees burned.

"Riley, are you okay?" Faith asked.

"My knees hurt." I rubbed my eyes. "What happened?"

Faith grabbed me up and put her face close to mine. "Shhh. I think you passed out. I caught you so you would not fall on your face." She put her arm around my shoulders and helped me to straighten up. "They are coming over. Try not to look like you just fainted."

"Huh? Oh ... okay."

"By the way," Faith whispered, "you beat four kids!"

The excited mob circled around me. Flip clicked pictures of my shoes. "Girl, you are one fast mzungu!"

Mom looked me in my eyes. "Do you need some water? *What* happened at the end?"

Faith pointed to the scrape on her forehead. "I guess it is a day for crashing."

"I think she was just being dramatic," Flip said. "Flinging herself across the finish line like they do in the Olympics. I'm glad you were wearing the Sole Fires. We may actually have all the pictures we need for the ads."

"You look a little pale." Fawn handed me a banana. Faith grabbed it and cracked it open for me.

Kiano wagged his finger at me. "You started out too fast, but with some training you could be a good runner."

"You did quite well," Jomo smiled.

I took a bite of banana, followed by a gulp of water. I wanted to say something clever, but my mind was a little foggy and my lips tingled, so I just nodded and said, "Yep."

Lorie Kipjabe spoke to the crowd from a megaphone, "We will give out the awards in ten minutes. Then everyone is welcome to come and swim in the pool at the training center."

Kids cheered and ran over to sit in the grass for the awards.

"We will go save a seat near the front." Kiano winked, and the group all headed toward the award ceremony. Faith and I stayed back and walked together.

"Thanks for helping me out over there," I said to Faith.

"It was my pleasure," she said. "It was brave of you to race Kenyan children."

"It was probably a little dumb too," I said. "I guess I

just don't like people telling me I can't do something." I rubbed my knees. "But in this case, they were probably right."

Faith shook her head. "No, they were not. You *did* do it! You were very determined."

I smiled. "You were too."

"Thank you. So I guess we have a very important trait in common?" She held up her hand for a high five.

"Yeah." I smacked her hand. "Let's go get your prize money."

As we walked over to the ceremony, I passed by some of the kids I had run with in my race.

"Congratulations, Mae Kiplabat," one of the boys said, and then he skipped in front of me.

"Hey, wait up!" I said to the kid.

He stopped and looked back at me. He had brown smudges on his lips and a smile on his face. "Yes?"

"Why did you call me that? My name is Riley Mae."

"Oh," he nodded. "The nice man who takes the pictures told us that was your name. He gave us chocolate, and said he would give us more if we let you run ahead of us to the finish line."

"WHAT?"

"He said you are a beginning runner, and that it would be very good if we let you beat us."

"But why would you do that? Wasn't it embarrassing to have a mzungu finish ahead of you?"

They all laughed and held up their chocolate candy bars. "We run every day. We do not get to have chocolate every day. We LOVE chocolate."

Well, at least they had their priorities straight.

I trudged over to the award ceremony and plopped down on the grass next to Faith. How did Flip know I was going to sneak into the race, and where did he find out the name Mae Kiplabat? I glanced over to where he was, at the side of the group, taking pictures. His camera lens scanned the crowd, and then I saw it stop on me. I acted out the words "I know you gave those kids chocolate so they would let me win." Flip pulled the camera away from his face, smirked in my direction, and gave me a thumbs-up.

Despite my humiliation over the race, I was still happy to watch Faith go up to collect her winnings. I didn't know exactly how much money one thousand shillings was, but I hoped it was enough for her to go to a good high school. But even if it wasn't, I was pretty sure she would figure out a way to get the rest. And I would certainly figure out a way to get Flip back for his chocolate deception.

Chapter 16

Dear TJ,

Have you ever passed out? I did today, and I wouldn't recommend it. It happened when I tried to run against a bunch of really fast kids in Kenya without being used to the elevation. Luckily, my friend Faith caught me before I fell on my face and broke my nose. That would have been just great, wouldn't it? A nose cast would go so nicely with the one that is still itching me to death on my right hand. I don't think I even told you about how I got that, did I? Let's just say that being a shoe spokesmodel has not been the safest job in the whole world. It's actually been a huge headache — kinda like the one I have right now which is not letting me sleep. I'm sure I got it from passing out, and like I said before, it's not a good idea.

If you see Rusty, tell her hi for me. I'm kind of worried about her. And if you see Sean, tell him that I haven't seen one single donut since I've been in Africa.

Have you been back to church yet? I think that would be a good idea.

Hope I get to come home soon.

Love, Riley

Istared at the letter I just wrote to my best friend. It seemed like forever since I had seen her. Last time we talked on the phone was when I was in Montana, and she was all excited that my birthday was coming up.

Lord, please let this crazy adventure be over soon so I can go home!

Faith must have noticed me rubbing my head while I wrote my letter to TJ.

"Riley, are you all right? Does your head hurt?" She closed the huge book she was reading and came over to sit next to me on my bed.

I lay down and rubbed my temples. "Yes. It's killing me."

Faith got up to pour me a glass of purified water that Lorie had brought us.

"Here. This will help." She handed me the glass and I drank it all down.

"Thanks." I glanced over at that huge book. "What were you reading?"

Faith cringed. "History."

"What for?"

"The KCPE tests. They will be here too soon, I am afraid."

"KCPE?"

"Kenya Certificate of Primary Education. I must pass the tests in order to move on to secondary school. That will be easy. But my scores must be very high so I can apply to a good school. It is very competitive."

"So ... you need money *and* brains too?"

She smiled. "Yes."

"I'm not sure I'd be able to do what you're doing."

"You would be able to do it. You are determined, remember?"

I laughed, remembering my silly little plan that tricked nobody.

"Maybe. I mean, I like school and everything. But I don't really have a reason to go crazy with studying."

Faith sat down on her bed, opened her book, and then stared out the window. "I want to be a doctor someday, so school is very important."

"Really, a doctor? That's amazing that you already know what you want to be."

Faith moved her opened book to the floor and lay down on her bed. She stared at the ceiling. "Many times when I was growing up in my village, someone was sick, and they could not get to a doctor. They would die. One day—when I was eight, I think—some missionary doctors came out to visit us at the village. My aunt Akeelah had been very sick, and they gave her medicine. She did not die! It was a miracle. You will meet her tomorrow, Riley. The day she was healed was the day I knew God wanted me to be a doctor."

"Wow. I wish I knew what I want to be when I grow up."

Faith smiled. "You will find out, at the right time. Someday, something special will happen, and you will hear God's voice guiding you toward what he wants for you. And when you hear it, you will study, run, work, or do whatever you have to do to become what he wants you to be. I know that being a doctor will bring God much pleasure."

Faith seemed so much older to me than twelve. And she was so far ahead of me in the area of life planning.

God, what do you want me to be?

Whatever it was, I hoped it would be in Fresno. And very soon.

So I closed my eyes and prayed a minute.

Lord, today was fun, and even though Africa is a little better than I thought it would be, I still miss my friends, and my church, and my Dad. Can you please make it so I can go home? I really do want to know what you want me to be when I grow up. But I'm too far away from home right now to figure it out . . .

I sighed, opened my eyes, and stared at the ceiling. Everything looked a little clearer, and my head felt better!

I sat up. "Hey, Faith!"

She sat up, startled. "What? Are you all right, Riley?"

"Yes. My headache is almost gone. What did you put in that water?"

She held her hands up. "Nothing. It was just water. And I prayed for your healing as you drank it."

"That's amazing." I rubbed my head. "You're gonna be a super-awesome doctor."

Faith smiled.

"Hey, since your prayers seem to work so fast, could you pray for me to go home soon?"

Faith frowned. "But I do not want you to go home! You have not visited my village yet. You must meet my Aunt Akeelah and Masara and all the children. It will be so fun to have you come to my house."

I placed the back of my hand on my forehead and threw my head back for dramatic affect. "Okay, okay. But you have to promise me that you won't let me contract malaria, or … what are some of those other diseases that swirl around here?"

"Oh," Faith said, matter-of-factly, "you mean yellow fever, dengue fever, typhoid, Rift Valley fever—"

"Stop. You're freaking me out."

Faith put her hand over her mouth. "Oh, I am sorry. I thought you really wanted to know. You do not have to worry, Riley. You have had immunizations and medication for most all of them. The only thing you may have to worry about is the dreaded traveler's diarrhea."

My mouth dropped open. Then I brushed it off. "Oh, well if *that's* all."

We both laughed, and I lay back down and prayed again.

God, get me outta here.

Chapter 17

As it turned out, Flip didn't get all the pictures he needed for the Swiftriver ad, so the next morning I had to return to the scene of my embarrassment with a fresh pair of Sole Fires and about fifteen different running outfits.

"Okay," Fawn said, "this will be a lot easier than yesterday. Hardly any running."

"Good." I bent at the waist to touch my toes. I grabbed the back of my right leg. "Ooh, I'm kinda sore."

"What?" Flip said. "How can the famous Mae Kiplabat be sore?"

I walked over close and stared him down. "HOW did you find out about Mae Kiplabat?"

Flip got a twinkle in his eye. "I can't say."

"You *have* to tell, or I may blame someone who is innocent, and I'm sure everyone is but you."

"Okay, I'll show you." Flip took his camera off the tripod and began clicking through his pictures. "Hmm ... where is that one?" He stopped and handed me the camera. "There. That should answer your question."

It was a picture of long-braids Mary handing me the number thirteen, right before I hid it in my pocket. Rats.

"After I saw that," Flip said, "I figured something was up, so I checked the registration list. There you were, number thirteen, under the name Mae Kiplabat."

"And then you paid those kids in chocolate so they would let me beat them? That was SO humiliating!"

He looked me straight in the eyes. "I was trying to *save* you from being humiliated."

I had to admit, Flip really was a caring goofball. I looked down at my feet and drew circles in the dirt with my Sole Fires, trying to figure out what to say.

Fawn came over and patted me on the shoulder. "Flip, do something to fix this. Our spokesgirl is all moody now."

Flip dropped to his knees in the dirt. "Shoe girl, I'm sorry. What can I do to make it all better?"

I thought about those happy, chocolate-smudged kids who let me win and came up with the perfect answer. "I would like one hundred chocolate bars, please."

"One hundred? Why on earth do you need that many?"

"Not sure. But Faith mentioned that a bunch of kids live in her village, so I might need them to make friends. It seems like chocolate works around here."

"You've got a point. But where am I going to get that many chocolate bars?"

"Oh, c'mon! You can probably afford to have someone do a flyover and drop them out of the sky or something." I pointed my thumbs to my chest. "Just make sure they hit Mae Kiplabat's pocket, okay?"

Flip stood, held out his hand and shook my cast. "It's a deal."

"Good," Fawn looked at her watch. "Now can we get back to the shoot? We've got a party to attend in an hour and I don't want to miss the chapati."

I found out why she didn't want to miss it later at Lorie Kipjabe's center. Chapati is way better than ugali! Unless, of course, you hate bread and butter and sugar and cinnamon. And that was just the "dessert" chapati. There was "dinner" chapati too—a bread which we wrapped beans in, and this thick meat stew. The lady runners seemed so excited to have the chapati. They told us that it isn't normally on the menu for them when they're training. I understood why after eating about six of them. All I felt like doing was lying down and eating more chapati. Running was the furthest thing from my mind.

Chapter 18

The next day was sort of sad, because we had to pack up and leave Lorie Kipjabe's training center. Even though it wasn't a fancy place to stay, I really felt welcomed by all the ladies, and I wished we had time to get to know them better.

Kiano and his family were excited to leave; it meant they were finally returning to their village after being gone for seventeen months. But it had been good for them to be in Montana, because Sunday was able to get treatments for his leukemia. And if we didn't need a peaceful place to hide out for a while, Kiano and his girls would probably still be there.

"It is my privilege to help," Kiano had said when he offered to take us home to his village. "I believe God wants me to do this."

There was no arguing with that.

"If they had a road here," I said, "it might make this trip a little less bumpy." Our Jeep bounced over rutted dirt and grass patches across random fields on the way to Kiano's village. I didn't think anyone heard me. So I spoke a little louder to Jomo, who was driving. He got stuck with me in the front seat again.

"Has anyone ever thought of putting a road in here?" The Jeep dipped hard to the left and I grabbed the handle on the door. "I think my headache is back."

Jomo smiled. "This is the road. And it is in better shape than usual."

I grabbed my head. "Oh, well that's good, I guess. But I hope that trailer doesn't fly off the back of Fawn's Jeep!"

I looked back and laughed as I saw the Jeep and trailer rocking back and forth in opposite directions of each other. "I think we should all just give up and walk."

"Most people *do* have to walk," Jomo said.

"It's going to be fine, honey," Mom was trying to balance a map on her lap in the back seat. "Now do you see why it was a good idea to go to Kiano's village for protection? No one will be able to sneak up on us—that's for sure."

I slumped down in the seat of the Jeep, wondering when someone would finally say that this nightmare was over and we could go home.

Soon we came upon a group of buildings with walls made of thick tree branches all bunched together, and roofs made of long grassy-looking stuff. The fronts of the buildings were open, so I stared in as we passed. There were cows in there, and other moving things. Then the road opened up into a large dirt circle—like a cul-de-sac—and surrounding the circle were round mud huts with the same grassy-looking roofs.

We had barely gotten out of the Jeeps when Kiano's family was mobbed by a wall of smiling adults and jumping kids. I laughed as I watched little Hope race out of the Jeep and escape through the crowd's legs. She ran to a little girl about her size and almost tackled her with a hug. She grabbed her hand and together they ran into one of the huts.

"Boy, that girl is quick to disappear," Flip said. He was standing next to me clicking pictures.

"Yeah," I said. "I hope there are no rhinos in there."

"Riley!" I turned to see Faith walking my way with an older, kind-looking woman with black hair in short, tight braids. "I would like for you to meet my Aunt Akeelah. She is my mother's sister. The one I told you about."

I stood up straight and tall. "Jambo." I didn't know whether to hold my hand with the cast out to shake hers, or to curtsy, or what.

I didn't have to think long, because she reached out her slender long arms and hugged me. "Jambo! Welcome to our village, Miss Riley Mae. We are so happy that God has brought you here. Are you hungry?"

I rubbed my stomach. "A little, I guess."

"Then come into my house. I have been cooking most of the day." When she saw our trailer, her eyes got wide. "Did you bring many things with you?"

I shrugged. "I only brought one suitcase. Oh—and another one full of shoes, which I sort of have to take everywhere I go. And besides water bottles, I'm not sure what else is in the trailer. It's supposed to be a surprise or something."

Akeelah smiled and looked around. "I like surprises. Today I was surprised by the return of my sister's family. Soon, I pray, my sister Ajia and nephew Sunday will return too."

It was weird thinking that Akeelah was Sunday's mom's sister. She looked at least twenty years older. "Sunday told me to tell everyone that he misses you and that he'll be home soon."

Faith shook her head. "My brother does not know what he is talking about. He still has a long way to go."

Akeelah frowned and patted Faith on the shoulder. "You must believe, my dear niece. We have been praying daily that God will heal him."

Faith sighed. "I know, and I want to believe. But leukemia is such a difficult disease. I studied about it while I was in Montana."

"And someday, when you are a doctor, you will help people with that illness. But for now, you must not worry."

Our little group easily filled up Akeelah's "kitchen" in the middle of her small house. We sat on benches in a circle around what looked like a round camping stove with some cooking pots surrounding it. Colorful rugs mostly covered the dirt floor. Akeelah asked Faith and Grace to help her dish some familiar-looking food onto plates, and they handed them to the men first and then to Mom, Fawn, Grace, and me.

Akeelah served herself some food, but then put her plate down on a bench and looked around. "Where is Hope?"

"With Johanna, of course," Grace said.

Akeelah shook her head. "Johanna really missed Hope. It was touching that she asked for her everyday even though she was not even three years old when Hope left."

"They are like sisters," Grace told me. "Born within a day of each other."

"I saw them go into one of the huts," I said. "But don't ask me which one."

"Playing dolls, I am sure," Kiano said. "When they are hungry they will appear."

I began to form the ugali into a spoon and then dipped it into the green veggie stuff which Akeelah said was made of kale and called "sukuma wiki."

"It means 'to stretch the week,'" Akeelah said. "The food fills us up and is healthy. It helps get us through the week."

I took a bite of some meat and liked it. "This tastes like chicken."

Kiano laughed. "It is chicken."

I sighed and relaxed. "Oh, good. So you have chicken here?"

Kiano pointed out the door to the hut. "Go, look outside."

I did. And I saw a few chickens running around loose. "Oh. Are those the ones you eat then?"

"When we can catch them," Akeelah said. "You can help us prepare the next one if you like."

Flip spoke up. "Riley would love that. She was just telling me the other day how she wanted to learn how to kill and pluck a chicken."

"Very funny," I said, taking another bite. It didn't taste quite as good to me that time.

Fawn took a sip of her drink. "This is good chai tea. Do you have many dairy cows?"

Akeelah nodded. "We are blessed in our village. The maize and tea crops are doing well this year too. Our prayer group has been asking for God to bless this area, and he has done it."

"Prayer group?" I said. "Do you have a church building here in your village?"

"We do not have one large enough to hold everyone," Akeelah said. "But we meet out in the circle for worship services on Sunday mornings. The women and the older girls meet on the other mornings for prayer before we go to collect water."

"Do you have a well nearby?" I asked.

"No," Faith said. "I wish we did."

I shot a confused glance toward Flip. "Can't you do something about that?"

"I'm working on it, kiddo. I was right in the middle of assembling a well-digging team three years ago when my dad was killed and all the court drama started. And then, I had to become Flip Miller, your superb photographer for Swiftriver shoes."

"All in God's timing," Akeelah said. "And while we wait, we have water sources about three kilometers away."

Faith nodded. "There's no road to the water, so everyone carries a container and we bring it back together."

"How often do you go?" I asked.

"Twice a day."

"Two times?" I think my mouth was hanging open.

"Yes."

"But what if you have school?"

"I go before and after school."

"Can the three of us go with you tomorrow morning?" Fawn gestured to me and Mom. "A couple extra hands would help, right?"

"You can come with us this afternoon," Akeelah said. "We have many dishes to wash, so the extra water will be helpful."

* * *

I don't know why, but I thought that the "water source" was going to be some kind of station with spigots—like when we go camping. So when I found out that we had walked thirty minutes to a muddy pond, I gasped.

"Why are we filling up jugs with this?" I turned to Faith and a few other pre-teen girls that had joined us for this job.

One of the girls named Rose spoke up. "It is the best we can do for now. During the rainy season we can collect cleaner water in our pots."

I put the jug up to my nose to sniff what I had just filled it with. "This stuff will make you sick." I was relieved that Flip had brought bottled water for us in the trailer.

Rose sniffed her water too. "Before three years ago we strained it and boiled it, but sometimes, yes, we did get sick. But then, Mr. Flip sent water purifiers to our village, so we are very fortunate."

Mom came over after filling her container. "Are you ready for the hike back? Akeelah wants to get the dishes and the kids washed up, and I want us to be all safe and secure before dark."

Another half hour walk was in front of us, but this time I had a jug of water to carry. Many of the women carried them on their heads, and I tried that for a minute until my neck started hurting. Some of the girls had round plastic drums that they rolled and kicked along the path. But most had the kind like I had—with a handle— and everyone had to keep shifting it from one hand to the other to keep from straining one arm too much. The problem with me was that I had that stupid cast on my right hand, so about halfway back to the village, my left arm felt like it was going to pull off my body.

"Owww." I set the jug down.

Fawn came up behind me and began massaging my shoulders. "How about you let me take that water for you?"

I examined the new blisters that were forming on my good hand. "Nah. I can do it. No one else gets to wimp out."

"Riley, you're not wimping out. You never could. It's not in your nature. Right now though, you *do* have to obey your personal assistant, who is insisting that you give up your jug. No argument. Case closed."

I sighed. "Thanks, Fawn."

"It's no bother." She shrugged her shoulders a couple of times as she picked up the water jugs. "Look at that," she grinned. "It kind of balances me out."

Chapter 19

By the time we arrived back at the village, I was exhausted and hungry, but the food was put away somewhere and the dishes were stacked up and ready to be washed. I was shocked at how fast the water disappeared with all the washing. Hope needed it the most. I guess she and Johanna had eventually come out of the hut and had a great old time playing in the dirt with sticks.

"I do not care if I am dirty!" Hope squirmed as Faith wiped her feet with a warm soapy rag.

"I care," Faith said. "I do not want dirt in our bed."

I looked around the hut that Kiano and his family called home. The whole thing was basically one room, but with free-standing room dividers that were just a little taller than me, made of branches that were tied together with some kind of tough plant strand. Between the walls were beds with very thin mattresses.

I pointed to the biggest bed in the room. "Is that where you guys sleep?" I asked Faith.

"Yes, all three of us. Although by morning I will probably be on the floor since Hope rolls around so much."

"But I am going to sleep at Johanna's house tonight, remember?" Hope wiggled some more as Faith tried to dry her feet with a towel.

"I do not know about that, Hope. There are already too many children in that house."

"Miss Masara said it was okay. Please, please, please ..."

Grace, who was reading on the bed, sat up and interrupted Hope. "Yes, Faith, you must let her go to Masara's, or we will not have any peace. Riley, are you going to stay with us tonight?"

Just then, Mom and Fawn came in with some suitcases. Where they were going to put them, I had no clue.

"Mom, where are we all staying tonight?"

"The guys are staying at Jomo's next door, and we girls will be in here."

I had almost forgotten about my bodyguard, Jomo. "He lives next door? Is he married?"

"His wife died," Grace looked down and frowned. "She was my favorite auntie."

"I'm so sorry, Grace," Fawn said.

"So Jomo lives alone?" I asked.

Faith shook her head hard. "No, he has three huge sons. There will not be much room for the men over there."

"It'll be okay," Fawn said. "Flip loves sleeping on the ground."

I laughed, imagining Flip trying to hop around with his cast in the crowded man hut.

"Can I go to Johanna's now?" Hope had collected a pink blanket and a baby doll from the "bedroom."

"I will take you and make sure it is okay." Faith grabbed Hope up and started to carry her out of the house.

Hope fought her a little. "I can walk!"

"You will get your feet dirty!"

Hope wiggled, but Faith was stronger. "Let me carry you, or you will not go."

"Bye, Hope!" Grace waved and seemed relieved to watch her baby sister being carried out the door.

Faith wasn't gone long. She and Akeelah came back a few minutes later. Akeelah carried in a plate of chapati.

She held it out to me. "I thought you might still be a little hungry."

It was perfect timing since my stomach was growling like a lion. I grabbed three pieces.

"Grace." Akeelah motioned to Grace, who was sitting on the bed. "Would you like to share your Bible story with all of us?" Grace had been reading for quite some time, but I didn't realize it was from the Bible.

"Yes, I would," Grace said, and she got up to join us in our circle, without her eyes ever leaving her book.

"I am reading about the prophet Jonah," Grace said. "God told him to go to the people who lived in the city of Nineveh. He wanted Jonah to tell them that God was going to destroy them because of their wickedness. But Jonah didn't want to go to Nineveh, so he ran away."

"He did not get very far, did he?" Akeelah closed her eyes like she was picturing the story in her mind.

"No," Grace said. "Jonah ended up in the belly of a big fish for three days, and while he was there, he prayed."

Grace held her Bible open with one hand, and gestured with the other, but her eyes stayed glued on the text.

"And then ... the fish spit him out onto dry land!"

Akeelah opened her eyes. "And what did Jonah do then, Grace?"

Grace finally looked up. "He went to Nineveh, of course. And the people listened to what he said, and they turned from their wicked ways, so God did not destroy them."

"That's a fun story, and it has a great ending," I said.

Akeelah stood. "Well, it was a good ending for the people of Nineveh, at least. But who really knows about Jonah?"

"What do you mean?" I asked.

Grace looked back down at her Bible again. "It says here that Jonah was very upset."

What? I got up and went over to look at the Bible with Grace.

She pointed to a paragraph and read straight from Scripture:

"When God saw what they had done and how they had put a stop to their evil ways, he changed his mind and did not carry out the destruction he had threatened. This change of plans greatly upset Jonah, and then he became very angry so he complained to the LORD about it."

I'd never heard that before. "He complained? Shouldn't he have been happy for the people of Nineveh?"

Akeelah closed her eyes again. "He was angry that the Lord showed mercy to sinners." She shook her head. "That should never be, since Jonah was a sinner too."

"Did he ever change his mind and become happy about it?" Faith asked.

Grace put her Bible down. "The Bible doesn't say." She shook her head. "Why doesn't it say, Auntie?"

Akeelah shrugged. "Maybe God wants us to think

about that and decide what might have happened to Jonah."

"Well," Grace said, "if he stayed angry, he probably became a mean old man."

"A mean old man who smelled like fish," I added.

Everyone laughed.

Grace's eyes lit up and she held a pointer finger up in the air. "I think a good ending would have been for him to stay with the people of Nineveh, to get to know them, and to like them. Maybe he would even fall in love with one of the women in Nineveh. Possibly a princess."

"Ooh, a love story!" Fawn said.

Grace continued, "Then maybe he would be happy that God saved them, and the story could end with Jonah praising and thanking God instead of complaining. And there would be a wedding, of course."

Faith smiled. "Grace, you should write that story."

"I am going to start right now." Grace took her Bible over to the bed, sat down, and pulled out a spiral notebook from her Disney princess backpack. She also took out a pen and began click, click, clicking it while she looked up at the ceiling.

"I think the princess will be named ... hmmmm ... Grace! Yes, Grace it is. And she will be the most beautiful girl in all the land. Jonah will fall in love with her the minute he sees her, but she will not like him at first because he smells like fish."

Then she sat up straight, frowning, and squinted back at us. "Can you see better over there? It always gets dark when I have the best ideas."

"I will be right back." Akeelah left the house, and a couple of minutes later we heard kicking on the door. Mom gestured for us all to stay put, and she cautiously approached the door. "Who is it?"

"It is Akeelah. My hands are full."

Mom looked relieved and opened the door. Akeelah carried a box that contained several orange lights. "Some people brought our village gifts while you were in the United States." She pushed a button on one of the lights and it spread a beautiful glow across the room. Then she gave one to each of us. "These solar lights have saved us from having to buy kerosene, and they are safer for us to have in the houses."

Grace grabbed hers and hugged it. "I can write all night!"

"It is perfect timing," Faith said. "I will be able to study for my KCPE exams into the evening now."

"Well, do not stay up too late and miss the morning prayer meeting. Bring your lights with you to my house at five." Akeelah gave each of us a kiss on the cheek and made her way to the door. "God bless you with a peaceful night's sleep."

Mom, Fawn, and I all stared at each other. I held my light up to my chin, so the glow would light my face. "Did she say FIVE?"

Chapter 20

"Riley, wake up."

I shot up from my bed and turned on my solar light. "What?" I rubbed my eyes. "Is everything okay?"

Mom appeared a little blurry on the other side of the big mosquito net that Faith, Grace, and I were sleeping under.

"Yes, everything's fine. But it's 4:45 and prayer starts in a few minutes."

I felt around in the bed for bumps that might be Faith and Grace, but there were none.

"They're already at Akeelah's. Come on." Mom lifted the net and handed me a hoodie. I threw it over my pajamas and pulled the hood up over my bed head. That's where I planned to keep it too.

We stepped out of the house and walked the few feet to Akeelah's. We knocked on the door.

"Who gets up this early?" I barely got those words out when a woman swung open the door to reveal a crowd of women and girls. Some stood against the walls and others sat on the floor. The oldest women sat on the benches that surrounded Akeelah's stove in the middle of the dimly lit room. There were even a few women sitting on the two beds at the back of the one-room house.

Mom elbowed me in the shoulder. "There's your answer. *Everyone* is up this early."

"Riley! Over here!" Grace and Faith sat against the far wall with a cozy blanket covering them. I was jealous of how nice and neat their tight cornrow braids looked.

"Hey, I didn't even hear you guys get out of bed." I slumped down the wall next to them and pulled some of the blanket over my legs.

"It was because you were snoring," Grace said.

"Grace!" Faith shook her head. "That is impolite to say to a guest."

"Really? I snored? Are you sure it was me? Maybe it was Fawn or my mom."

"It was in my ear," Grace said, as she rubbed her ear.

"Oh. I'm sorry. I didn't think I was a snorer. Maybe it's just an Africa thing."

"Well," Grace said, "we will pray that it is only a one-night thing."

Akeelah began singing something unfamiliar, but soothing, and the whole group except Mom, Fawn, and me sang along. The song ended just in time—before I drifted back to sleep.

"Good morning, ladies. We have some special guests from the United States who will be staying with us for a while. Please, if you can, speak in English during our prayer meetings. And maybe they can teach us a worship song in English?" Akeelah looked at me, and I tried to hide under my hood.

She laughed, "Next time, perhaps."

For the next hour, women prayed. Sometimes it was just one, but other times it was several at once. Even the girls my age prayed out loud. I looked up a couple of times, and each time my eyes met Fawn's. I remembered Flip had told me that Fawn stopped going to church when she was about my age, and he never asked her why. I wondered if she had ever been in a prayer meeting like this one. I know I hadn't.

Faith prayed for God to help her pay for a good school and for help to get good grades on her KCPE exams. Grace prayed for her mom, who was still in Montana with Sunday. Akeelah prayed for health for her family and for all the children in Masara's houses to feel the love of their heavenly Father, since they were orphans. That one got to me. Was Hope's friend Johanna an orphan?

The hour flew by, and Akeelah said the final amen. The women streamed out of the house in seconds.

"Well, I guess they didn't want to hang around to meet us," I said.

"Oh, no, it is not that." Faith gathered up her blanket and draped it around her shoulders. "They must go and collect water and firewood now, before the day's work begins."

"Do we have to go too?" I wasn't ready to trudge back out to the muddy pond so soon.

"We could. I usually do. But it is Monday, and school is today. I thought you might like to come with me."

Chapter 21

"School? You want me to come with you to school? In Kenya?"

"Why not? I do not think a mzungu student has ever come to our school before."

"Great. So I'd be like a circus sideshow or something?"

"A what?"

"Never mind." We walked the few steps back to Faith's house, and the girls immediately changed into their school uniforms.

"I am nervous to return to my class." Grace buttoned up her white blouse and tucked it into her dark blue skirt. "It has been a long time, and now I am in standard four."

"At least you do not have to worry about getting into a good high school yet," Faith said. She looked like she was struggling to button her skirt.

"I have an extra uniform, Riley," Faith said. "Would you like to try it on? I think we are about the same size."

"I don't know. I'm not even sure Mom will let me go—"

Just then, Mom and Fawn walked in from outside. They were eating something that looked like fruit.

"So, it's all set, Riley," Mom said. "Jomo is going to go

with you girls to school so you don't have to be bored here all day while Grace and Faith are gone."

"Isn't that great, Riley?" Fawn's eyes brightened as she slurped some more of what now looked to be a mango. "I think you should start to journal your experiences here. It would be very interesting to preteens back home."

Faith handed me a blouse and a skirt. "We will need to leave pretty soon if we are to make it on time."

How could that be? The sun was barely up. "What time does school start?"

"Seven-thirty," Faith said. "And remember, we have to walk a little ways to get there."

Fawn laughed. "Maybe Mae Kiplabat would like to run instead!"

"Uh, no thanks." I wasn't interested in passing out today.

I started to put on the blouse, but then stopped mid-button. "I can't believe I'm doing this." I closed my eyes and shook my head. "It seems like a crazy dream." I opened them back up. Nope, this was all real. "Will I even understand anyone?"

"Lots of the day will be in English," Grace said. "And all of the kids know English."

"I will help you understand." Faith helped me button my skirt.

"Can you do my hair like yours?"

"Not today," Faith said. "It would take too long. We will do it soon. But I warn you, it will hurt a little."

"I don't care. I just don't want to think about combing it out every morning if I'm going to be getting up so early."

A knock sounded at the door. It was Jomo. "I will be waiting for you girls in the circle when you are ready to go to school."

I was dressed, but I wasn't ready. I never thought I would start eighth grade in Africa!

"What shoes should I wear?" My flaming orange Sole Fires were the only shoes I had in the house. The rest were packed in the trailer somewhere. "Will these pass dress code?"

"They will be fine," Faith said, and she laced up her Sole Fires. "I think I am ready."

The girls strapped on their backpacks and we walked out to the circle to meet Jomo. He was sitting on an interesting bicycle that, on second glance, looked more like a motorcycle. Jomo handed me a helmet.

"Riley!" Grace laughed. "You have a boda boda to take you to school!"

"Jomo, can't I walk with them?" I turned around and saw Flip coming out of Jomo's house with his camera and a backpack. Great.

"Oh, good, you haven't left yet." Flip grabbed me by the arm and pulled me over a few feet. "I have something for you." He handed me the backpack. "School supplies. Don't leave them in the sun." He started to walk away, and then turned back, smiled, and waved. "Don't worry, I've got more."

Jomo fired up my motor-bicycle taxi. "Would you like to run or ride?"

"Are those my only two choices?"

Faith looked at her watch. "If we leave now, we might be able to walk fast and make it."

"Okay, then. I would like to walk fast." I took off toward the "sort of" road that had led us into the village the day before.

"Not that way." Grace pointed in the opposite direction. "The road to school is on the other side of the maize."

"A maze? Terrific. I'll get lost for sure. One time I got stuck in a hay maze for twenty minutes and I had to climb up to the top and wave for someone to rescue me."

Faith took off walking. "It is not a maze! It is *maize*."

I gave Faith a funny look. She led us through the tall, familiar-looking crops.

"Corn," she said.

Maize is corn. And of course, when you are in Kenya, you hike through the corn to get to school! Or maybe you jog, because that's what Faith started to do. "I do not want to be late on my first day back."

I slung the backpack over my shoulders and pumped my arms a little to keep up. The road we followed was much like the one we used to travel to the village—rutted and uneven. I could hear Jomo's boda boda following not too far behind us, and I prayed that I wouldn't get tired and have to hop on the back.

My prayer was answered—with a no—ten minutes later, when I was totally out of breath. I would ride the boda boda.

Jomo offered me a hand and I swung my leg over the back of the seat behind him. I stuffed my head into the helmet and held on tight to the handles on the side of the seat. Jomo hit the gas to catch up with a group of kids, who were all-out running to school.

"This is going to be like the circus is coming to town, isn't it?"

Jomo laughed and shook his head. "Oh, no. These children have seen plenty of elephants and lions."

"But how often does a mzungu, riding a boda boda in a Kenyan school uniform and bright orange running shoes show up?"

"Never," Jomo laughed. "This will be better than the circus."

I was relieved that Flip and his camera had stayed back at the village.

Chapter 22

I hoped that all the kids would be in the school building by the time my group arrived. Nope. Instead, they all lined the street and waved as we pulled up to the gate. My heart pounded. I felt like Santa Claus at the end of a Christmas parade. I was glad that I at least had the helmet on to cover my light-haired head.

Whatever happens, just smile, Riley. Pretend it's a photo shoot.

Faith ran over to help me off the boda boda. She grabbed my hand and didn't let go as we walked toward the line of about forty children that soon formed a ball right in front of me.

"Hi." I smiled and waved.

They all smiled while they stared at me.

"Oh … um, how about this … Jambo?" I smiled and waved again.

Some of the little ones yelled back, "Jambo!"

I kept smiling and whispered nervously to Faith through my teeth, "What should I say now?"

She spoke to the group, "This is my friend Riley Mae. She lives in the United States of America. She came with us today to see what Kenyan school is like."

An older girl with big, beautiful eyes and very short hair stepped forward. "I like your shoes."

"Riley is a shoe model," Grace said. "She is in magazines!" She dug an *Outdoor Teen Magazine* out of her backpack and held up the picture of me in my Rock Shocker hiking boots climbing Half Dome in Yosemite. The kids gathered around to see it.

"This is our chance to escape," Faith said, and she pulled on my hand and led me through the gate and into a dirt courtyard. She stood there for a minute, looking at three doors. "I do not know which classroom I am assigned to."

A woman in a white blouse and red skirt came out of one of the doors. She stopped and looked shocked for a moment when she saw me, but then she saw Faith and walked over to hug her. "You are home!"

She pulled back and smiled at Faith. "Oh my," she said with a loving tone. "You are beautiful, just like your mother. How is your brother?"

"He was doing fine for a while, but now there is a setback," Faith said. "Mrs. Kipsang, I would like for you to meet my friend Riley Mae. Riley, Mrs. Kipsang was my teacher for standard six. That is the last time I was at this school."

"And now we have fewer teachers, so I teach standard six through eight. I am afraid our classroom will be much more crowded than you remember it, but the good news is that I will be able to help prepare you for the KCPE exams."

"I have been studying," Faith said. "But I am anxious, since I have been away for so long."

"Do not worry," Mrs. Kipsang gently took Faith's hand and patted it. "You are a hardworking girl." Then she turned to me. "It is nice to meet you, Riley Mae."

"Nice to meet you too."

"I see you are in uniform." She raised her eyebrows. "Have you enrolled in our school?"

"Oh, no. I'm just visiting Faith's family, and they thought it would be fun if I came to school too."

"Can Riley sit with me during the lessons today?"

"Of course. Riley, you can help us learn what it is like to be a pupil at an American school."

"Okay, sure. We don't call ourselves pupils though. We're students."

"And are you a good student?"

"I'm pretty good. Not as good as Faith, though. I just need to study harder, I guess."

"There she is!" Some kid called out from the approaching crowd of "pupils."

Mrs. Kipsang turned her head to look at them. "Oh my. I am afraid that the children will be quite curious about you." She smiled. "If you would like to avoid their stares and questions, you may go into the classroom right now." Mrs. Kipsang pointed to the middle of the three doors.

This time, I grabbed Faith's hand and we both jetted into the room.

"Whew. That was close!"

Faith chose a desk in the front row of the small but tidy classroom and began unloading her books. "Yes, for now you have avoided them. At morning break—when we all go outside—then we will have to figure out what to do."

I pulled a chair up to Faith's desk and hung my backpack on it. Then I remembered about the mysterious school supplies Flip put in there. I zipped open the center pouch and laughed, remembering how he had told me not to leave them in the sun. The pack was filled with chocolate bars!

"Faith! I think I have an idea."

Chapter 23

Morning lessons were easy, since we were studying English. I didn't raise my hand to answer anything, because I was a visitor and all. Once in a while, I turned around to look at the kids who were jammed in the little room, and each time they were all staring at me. A few were standing in the back of the classroom, and I wanted to kick myself for taking an extra chair.

Faith was clearly the best student in class. She raised her hand to answer every question. I wondered if she could outscore me on an English test. Probably. But I was excited about that since Faith needed excellent scores to get into the national high school.

Morning break came at ten o'clock, and like we figured, all the kids searched for the mzungu in the orange shoes. This time I was ready for them.

"Jambo!" I said as I waved and held up my backpack. "I brought something special for all of you today. One of my favorite things!" The crowd moved in a little closer. I pulled out a chocolate bar, unwrapped it, sniffed it, and rubbed my stomach.

"Chocolate! Yum!" a little girl yelled and ran up and hugged my waist. A bigger girl—probably her sister— came up to pull her off me.

"It's okay," I said. "She can help me pass them out." The little girl smiled and led me over to a bench. "You can use this as a table and I will line everybody up."

She turned to the crowd, hands on her hips. "You must all have good manners or you will not get any." I giggled a little watching her wag her finger at the crowd of kids who were mostly older and bigger than she was. They listened to her though, and fell into line just as she had directed. A take-charge kid. I liked her.

Faith helped me pass the chocolate bars out while each kid told me their name. At the end there were two whole bars left. I saved one to give to Mrs. Kipsang, and I gave the other whole one to my new little friend.

"Thank you so much!" She hugged me again.

"You are welcome. I like people who like chocolate. What is your name?"

"Britney." She popped her first piece of chocolate into her mouth and began to unwrap the extra bar I gave her.

"Well, Britney, you should save this extra chocolate bar for later."

She frowned. "Why?"

"Because it has lots of sugar in it and you don't want it to affect your concentration in class."

"What does that mean?"

I knelt down to help her rewrap the candy bar and put it in her pack. "Well, when I eat too much sugar, it makes me crazy and I can't sit still. If that happens to you, your teacher won't like it."

Behind me I heard whooping and hollering and lots of

laughing. The boys had begun playing soccer with some sort of homemade ball. It looked like fun.

"Can we go play with them?" I asked Faith.

She gave me a serious look. "No."

I sighed. Never tell a sporty girl she can't play.

"Riley Mae? Would you like to play with *us*?" I turned to find three girls holding a dusty Coke bottle.

"Sure! What's the game?"

"Here." A short, but older-looking girl handed me the Coke bottle and led me out to the middle of the courtyard.

Faith followed close behind. "Riley, I do not think you will want to play this game."

I turned and whispered over my shoulder to her. "It'll be okay, Faith. This is all part of my plan to make friends."

Faith bit her index finger. "Oh, dear." Then she stepped back, as about fifteen girls formed a big circle around me. I still held the Coke bottle. I sort of wished it was a real Coke since I was getting a little thirsty.

The short girl yelled out to me. "This is how we play. When you are ready, say go, and then fill up the Coke bottle with dirt all the way to the top."

"Is that all?" I asked. "Do I have a time limit?"

Another girl called out, "You can take all the time you want, but as soon as you get hit with the ball, you are out."

Wait ... what?

"Excuse me," I said while holding up my good hand. "What ball are we talking about here?"

One of the big girls held up a homemade plant-like mushball, similar to the one the boys were kicking around.

"Is there only one ball?"

"Yes. We will be throwing it at you while you fill the bottle."

"SERIOUSLY?"

They all laughed, but they *were* serious.

"I told you," Faith said, with a concerned look on her face.

Little Britney yelled from the circle, "You can do it, Riley Mae! They have very bad aim."

I stood there for a minute wondering if they asked me to play because they liked me or because they hated me. This was just like dodgeball back home, but with a huge disadvantage!

But at least the ball looked soft. And I *never* back down from a challenge.

"GO!" I yelled.

The first thing I did was stare down the girl with the ball. Her eyes widened. She wound up and heaved the ball at my head. I ducked, and the ball missed me! The cool part was that the ball flew way outside the circle and another girl had to go chase it down.

Time to grab a handful of dirt. I tried to pour it in the bottle, but it was tough since I was keeping one eye on the super-fast girl as she retrieved the ball. She was back in a flash.

"Throw it, Tabitha!" one of the other girls yelled.

Tabitha held the ball awkwardly and took a long time

to wind up, so I scooped up another handful of dirt and poured it in the bottle.

Tabitha gave a weak throw, so the ball was easy to dodge. But I didn't have time to pick up dirt this time because one of the scary girls from the other side of the circle grabbed the ball. Uh-oh.

"AAAAAHHHHHH!" She brought the ball back behind her head with both of her hands and flung it forward.

I hit the deck, and she missed by a mile! And now I had more dirt in my mouth than was in the Coke bottle. I pushed myself up on my knees and got two handfuls of dirt in the bottle before one of the older girls finally came sprinting back to the circle with the ball.

"Nina!" the short girl yelled. "Do not throw so hard. She is winning!"

The Coke bottle was halfway filled. I smiled, brushed the dirt off my hands, and stood staring at the girl with the ball, ready to bolt. Just like when I'm in a pickle between the bases in a softball game.

The next girl threw at my feet. I grunted, and jumped just high enough for the ball to go under me. I turned back around. Nina had the ball again.

"Oh, no!" I yelled.

She quickly took the ball back with one hand, and raised her opposite leg just like a baseball pitcher. Should I jump right or left?

I chose left.

She growled again. I jumped. And it was the right choice. The ball flew away again.

"Nina!" One of the girls stomped her foot and then

turned to retrieve the ball. Thankfully, she took her time, and I managed to get two more handfuls of dirt in the bottle. The level was now just over the top of the Coke label.

As I watched the girl return with the ball, loud clapping and cheering started behind me.

It was the boys.

"Riley Mae! Riley Mae! Riley Mae!"

I wanted to turn around and see what was going on, but I had to stay focused on this little girl with the ball.

She smiled at me innocently, and then she took the ball in both hands, squatted low, and threw the ball underhanded into the middle of the circle—like she was trying to make a free throw in basketball.

I grabbed the bottle and ran to one side of the circle. I scooped up a handful of dirt before the ball dropped in the center.

I eyeballed the girls to see which one would come in after it. Of course, it was Nina.

"Give someone else a chance!" one of the boys yelled. Then I heard more "Riley Mae, Riley Mae!" cheers coming from around the circle. I grabbed one more handful of dirt. Nina ran back to her position in the circle.

She pulled the ball back with two hands again ...

I looked down at the Coke bottle, opened my hand, and poured in the last bit of dirt ...

And the mushball smacked me on top of the head.

"Owwwwww."

Okay, so it wasn't as soft as I thought. I rubbed my head and tried to stand. A couple of girls reached out to help me up. Kids cheered and mobbed me. I think I heard someone ringing a bell somewhere. Or maybe that was just in my head.

"That was so good, Riley! You won!" Little Britney brought me a tin cup with some water. I raised it to my lips, but Faith grabbed it away from me.

"Do not drink that! You will get that problem we discussed."

I rubbed my head again. *The traveler's diarrhea.* "Oh, yeah. Thanks, Doc."

Faith guided me over to a bench to sit down. "You are very dirty," she said.

I looked down at the uniform Faith had loaned me. "I'm so sorry. I'll clean it, I promise."

Another bell rang, and thankfully I found out that it was a real bell. Mrs. Kipsang held it in her hand and yelled out to the group of kids, "One minute until class resumes!"

"Oh, boy." I took a deep breath and rubbed my head again.

Big scary Nina jogged over to the bench. She reached out her hand to help me up.

"Thanks," I said.

"You are welcome. That was an exciting game."

"That's for sure. You throw hard. We could use you on our softball team back home."

Nina smiled and put her arm around me as we walked back to the classroom.

"I am glad you have come to our school, Riley Mae. Is it okay if I sit next to you in class?"

I shrugged. "Sure."

As we settled in our chairs, I leaned over to Faith. "See, my plan to make friends worked." I raised my eyebrows up and down.

Faith just laughed and shook her head.

Chapter 24

A rt class was next, and though I can barely draw a stick figure, I really enjoyed it. Mrs. Kipsang—who had to teach all the subjects for three grades—played some quiet music with a nice beat, and we worked with orange, yellow, and red watercolors to paint an African sunset.

"Everyone's paintings are so beautiful compared to mine," I said, as we hung them up to dry. We had to stand on chairs and clothespin them across a line that was strung above our heads between two walls.

"Maybe you have not had a chance to see and appreciate an authentic African sunset yet," Mrs. Kipsang winked. "You will improve."

At eleven-thirty, the students all gathered their belongings and flew out the door.

I looked at my watch and then at Faith. "Is it lunch time already?"

"Yes, so we should hurry."

"Do you have a cafeteria or something? We didn't bring a lunch with us."

"What?" Her eyebrows crinkled up, but then her face relaxed. "Oh … you do not remember, do you?"

"Remember what?"

"We go home for lunch."

"All the way home?"

Faith smiled and nodded.

I looked at my watch again. "When do we have to be back?"

"In our seats, ready to go, at two o'clock."

I grabbed my backpack. "Then we better get moving! I'm a slow runner, you know."

We started jogging as soon as we got out the door. Jomo had fired up the boda boda and watched as I passed him. "Don't worry," I yelled back. "I'll be climbing on in just a little bit. I want to train my feet a little first!"

Lunch went by fast. Akeelah had made us a yummy meal called githeri. It was basically corn and beans, and it really filled me up. Faith and Grace took a fifteen minute nap, but I wasn't tired, so I told everyone the story about how I shared the chocolate bars and about my hilarious adventure playing the Coke bottle game.

"I can't wait to teach it to our softball team when we get home," I said. "It could help improve our speed for running bases. I've gotta figure out how they made that ball, though."

"I am sure they used sisal strands," Kiano said.

"Sisal?"

"Yes." Kiano pointed in the distance. "The sisal plants are the ones that look like huge pineapples. The rope strands have many uses here in the village. I can show you how to make a ball later."

"How about now?"

Chapter 24

Then I heard Jomo starting up the boda boda over at the dirt circle.

I rubbed my stomach. "Uh-oh. I think I ate too much."

"Yeah," Flip said. "Good luck with the run back to school."

I smacked him on the shoulder. "I can't wait till you get that ankle cast off and have to run."

I jogged halfway back to school on my full stomach before climbing onto the boda boda. Then to my surprise, during History class, my stomach started growling! There wasn't an afternoon break, either. But finally, four-thirty came, and this time the kids ran out the door even quicker than at lunch.

"If they run very fast, they will have time to play before evening chores begin," Faith said.

I rode the boda boda the whole way this time, since my legs felt like Jell-O and I didn't want to hold Faith up. Grace was just a little way behind us, running with some of her friends.

"How many kids live in your village?" I yelled up to Jomo.

"Many. And most without parents."

"Why?"

"Many diseases plague us, and we lack proper medical care. My wife died of malaria. I pray to God every day that I will stay healthy for my children."

I watched as many of the kids ran ahead of the boda boda, and I wondered which ones didn't have parents. The thought sort of overwhelmed me. How did they survive from day to day? I was having trouble lately just being separated from my dad.

"So who is Masara?" I asked.

Jomo looked back and smiled. "Masara is my daughter!"

"You have a grown daughter?"

"Yes. She is twenty, and she loves children. She began taking care of the orphans in our village when she was sixteen. Soon there were too many, so I built her four houses. She cares for twenty-four children so far."

"So far?" I did the math. That was six children to a house. But only one Masara.

"Where does she sleep?"

"She sleeps in the house with the little ones, like Johanna. Then in the other houses, she has appointed an older child to keep watch over the others during the night. Akeelah cooks for the children, all day long."

I had no words. So for the rest of the ride, I counted the children who were running toward the village. As I counted, I prayed.

Lord, is that one an orphan? Please help him to know that you are his heavenly Father.

Lord, what about that one? She looks so serious. Does she have a mom to hug her when she gets home today?

Lord, is that one in charge of a whole house of kids? Please help her not to be afraid when she hears noises tonight.

I kept praying and soon tears welled up and spilled onto my cheeks. Thankfully, since I was riding the boda boda, the wind dried them quickly. As we entered the village circle, I watched carefully as the different children ran to their houses, and almost all of the ones I had prayed for ran into Masara's children's homes.

Lord, you really need to answer my prayers!

"Thanks for the ride, Jomo. I mean ... thanks for the many rides." I swung my leg over the boda boda and hopped down.

"It is my pleasure. I will be here tomorrow for you if you would like to attend school again."

I hadn't even thought about tomorrow at all. I'd been too busy surviving today.

"Well, I might go, depending on what Mom says. The kids were nice and I learned some new things about Kenya. But I really hope she's going to tell me it's time to go home."

Jomo smiled. "I understand, and I will pray for that too. I am sure it is very hard for a young girl like you to be in such a different culture."

"Yes, I guess it is." I turned to go meet Faith and Grace inside their house. I hoped my mom was in there. I planned to give her a hug and tell her I love her.

Chapter 25

Water. I'd never given much thought to it until recently. I usually let gallons of it run down the drain while I wait for it to warm up for my shower. I flush a ton of it down the toilet several times a day. And when I drink from the purified water that comes out of the door of my refrigerator, I never wonder if it's going to make me sick.

But, here in this village in Kenya, every drop was valuable. And all those drops together were really heavy too.

This time as I carried my jug back to the village, I could feel my skin pinching under the handle, causing another blister to rise up on my palm under my middle finger.

"Do you want me to carry it for you?" Fawn reached out to grab the jug away, but something in me wanted to keep it this time.

"Nah, I got it. Thanks."

"Okay," she smiled. "See you up the road."

My stomach growled and I sped up my steps, knowing that the sooner we all got back to the village, the sooner we could eat.

I caught up to Faith, who carried a big container of water on her head.

"Faith, do you know what Akeelah is making for dinner tonight?"

Faith frowned. "I am sorry, but I think it is ugali and sukuma wiki again."

"Sounds great to me, actually. My stomach is an empty pit right now."

Faith smiled, "You have been very active since yesterday."

"Yes, but *you* are active all the time! Don't you ever get tired? I mean, there's so much walking, and fine—so you get water tonight, but then you have to get it again tomorrow. How do you keep it up?"

Faith and I walked along together for a minute or so before she answered. "It is hard to say. Part of it must be because it is what I have always done. But it is difficult and it can be dangerous. Sometimes the young women are kidnapped on the road by men from other villages." Faith frowned. "They are looking for wives to do all of their hard work for them."

I gasped, "What? That's horrible! I think I would just give up and die of thirst instead."

Faith smiled, "No, you would not." She held up a fist. "You are determined, just as I am. And everyone you see here would be helping you not to quit."

I looked around at all the women and young girls who were working so hard to take care of their families.

Faith continued, "We have a saying in Kenya that goes like this: 'If you want to go fast, go alone. If you want to go far, go together.'"

"I like that. Ha! You sure are fast by yourself."

"Yes, for races, that is good. But I would never make it living in the village alone. We need everyone. And today I need you too, Riley. Thanks for helping with the water. I am pretty sure that Hope will need a good washing again tonight."

We both laughed.

"Well, I have to admit, the last place I wanted to go was Africa. But it's been sort of fun. It's really different though. It seems that you spend most of your time just surviving. I can see why you like school so much now."

Faith nodded, "And I really appreciated having you come to school with me. I know it sounds silly, but I was nervous going back today. Your chocolate and watching you play that silly game helped me take my mind off my worries about my studies."

"Glad I could help. I guess." I giggled and rubbed the top of my head.

We arrived back at Akeelah's just as she was serving the sukuma wiki. I gobbled it up without one complaint about the veggies. I even ate an extra helping.

Darkness was closing in, so we quickly cleaned dishes and kids, and tonight I had to clean myself! I took what Mom always calls a "spit bath," with a soapy rag and some water that Akeelah warmed over her stove. It felt amazing.

"You're not tired yet?" I asked Faith, who was studying by the glow of her new solar light.

"No. I had a nap earlier, remember?"

"Are you kidding? How can fifteen minutes make that much difference?"

Chapter 25

"I do not know. It just does. You should try it tomorrow."

Tomorrow. The thought of it made me tired, so I fell asleep.

Chapter 26

Riley, wake up!"
I sat up. "What? Oh no, is it almost five? No, I ... I can't." I yawned and lay back down.

Mom swatted me on the behind. "At least come to prayer. You can decide about school later."

Grace and Faith were already gone, probably saving our place by the wall at Akeelah's. I hauled myself out of bed and reached for my solar light to help me find my hoodie in my opened suitcase at the foot of the bed.

Under the hoodie was my Bible. I grabbed it and took it with me to the prayer meeting. I got there right in the middle of a song, "Everything is Possible." One of the ladies would sing a line, and then all of us would echo back. We did the song several times, and each time the women sang louder and with more feeling.

"Today we are blessed to have Masara with us, to give us an update on the children." Akeelah stepped aside and a young smiling woman with long braided hair kissed Akeelah on the cheek. "Thank you, Auntie." Then she spoke to all of us.

"Good morning. First, I want to say that everyone is doing well right now—no sickness."

A bunch of ladies yelled, "Praise God!"

"So my prayer request is that you would ask God to heal the broken hearts of these young ones. Often, I hear crying in the night, and I wonder if they are thinking about their mothers and fathers. I am not able to comfort all of them every time they need it. I ask that you would pray that they all would come to know Jesus as their Savior early in their lives. He promises not to leave them as spiritual orphans."

Many of the women shouted "Amen" to that.

And then they started praying all together. I heard prayers for kids with all sorts of beautiful-sounding African names, and then I heard a few familiar American names. The name I heard the most was Johanna, maybe because Faith and Grace were praying out loud for her while they were sitting on both sides of me. I closed my eyes and tried to concentrate enough to form a silent prayer of my own, but instead of hearing my own words in my head, I heard something else:

Riley, I want you to help me answer their prayers.

I popped my eyes open and looked around. Faith and Grace were still praying out loud, so it hadn't been either one of their voices that I heard. Plus, it wasn't a girl's voice; it was more like a deep whisper in my heart. But there was no doubt what the words had been.

Then the room got quiet. Women were still praying with their eyes closed, but it was like someone hit a mute button on a TV remote control, because there was no more talking. I felt as if there were no more human words—whether in English, Swahili, or Kalenjin—that could adequately express what we were feeling for these children. We all stayed silent for what seemed like a long, long time. I felt like God was right there in the room.

And then there was sobbing. I looked up.

It was coming from Fawn.

Mom, Akeelah, and Masara moved over and put their hands on Fawn, and I saw Masara whisper something to her. Fawn nodded, and Masara hugged her.

Akeelah then opened her front door and motioned for the group to leave. Mom caught me on the way out. "Go ahead and get ready for school."

I nodded, and headed back to the hut, even though I wanted to stay and ask questions about Fawn. Clearly something had upset her enough that she couldn't maintain control in the prayer meeting. That's just not Fawn.

Chapter 27

After I put on my school uniform, I snuck over to the hut where Flip and the guys were staying. I tapped on the door and to my surprise it flung open. It was dark inside. And quiet, which didn't seem normal for a hut full of boys.

"Hello? Anybody here?" I stepped in a couple of feet, and just about concluded that nobody was home, when a rug on the floor began moving toward me.

"ROOOOOOAAAR!" The rug grabbed me by the foot and I screamed.

Then the rug laughed.

"Flip?" I kicked the "rug," which was really Flip's sleeping bag. "You almost gave me a heart attack! You know I have issues ever since the Herod-the-bear incident."

Flip stuck his head out and static caused his hair to stick up all over the place. He tried to smooth it down, but it didn't work. "Oh, yeah. Didn't mean to traumatize you." He scratched his fingers over his beard stubble. "What are *you* doing in the man hut?"

"I came for more chocolate. Mom's sending me to school again today."

Flip stood and shook the sleeping bag off. He walked

over to a suitcase and opened it. It was full of chocolate bars.

I looked around the dark hut that smelled like boy sweat. "So where are these huge sons of Jomo?"

"They're out feeding the cows and stuff like that. They left awhile ago. I wanted to help, but ..." He held up his foot with the cast.

"Shouldn't your foot be healed by now? You've had that thing on there forever."

"You too." He pointed to my cast. "Yours is starting to look brown instead of orange."

"Well, I'm not allowed to get it wet, so I can't clean it, and if you haven't noticed, there's a lot of dirt in Africa. Maybe we should fly back home to Fresno so I can get a new one. I'd rather have my birthday there anyway."

Flip wrinkled up his forehead. "Riley Mae Hart, I'm surprised at you! It's summer, and you're having the adventure of a lifetime. What's at home that is more exciting than all this?" He pointed around the hut.

"Friends, family, school, softball, stores, restaurants ..."

"But what about elephants, monkeys, and giraffes?"

"I haven't seen one single monkey yet."

"You will. And it's sure to be thrilling." Flip turned and reached into his suitcase. "How many of these do you want?"

I opened my backpack. "Just fill 'er up."

He grabbed a few of the chocolate bars and tossed them in. Then he unwrapped one and started having breakfast. "Hey, I have a great idea! How about I come to school with you and take pictures today?"

"No! It's already *almost* a circus when I show up. Bringing a clown would make it one for sure."

He chuckled. "Come on. Puhleeeeeese?"

He gave me that stupid Flip grin which made me almost say yes, but thankfully, Grace saved me from making that mistake when she flew into the man hut, grabbed me by the hand, and dragged me out the door.

"We have to go now!"

I had totally forgotten that their schedule left no room for hanging out and talking.

Jomo was waiting on the boda boda. I jumped on right away this time, so we wouldn't be late. By the time we got to school, pretty much all the kids had arrived and they had lined the street again. This time, instead of trying to hide, I just gave them my best princess parade wave.

The morning was stress free, with the English classes again. At the morning break, everyone wanted to play Coke bottle, but this time, since the top of my head was still tender, I chose to be a thrower instead of a bottle filler and human target. I also promised to give them all chocolate as they were on their way home for lunch.

"I may not have any more after today," I said to the crowd. "Will you let me hang out with you anyway?"

"Oh, yes! You are nice," little Britney said, wrapping her arms around my waist. "I want to you to stay forever!"

"Well, it won't be that long, but maybe I'll be here a few more days."

* * *

Two weeks later, I was still going to school, and I had

learned almost all of the kids' names! The running got easier, and I actually could make it all the way to school in the morning, and then home at night, but I rode the boda boda for lunch and back. I even developed a little circle of best friends: three girls—Tabitha, Emily, and believe it or not, Nina. Most days, we sat in a little circle during our morning break and talked. Faith always joined us, but she studied instead of taking part in the conversation. One day, we got permission from Mrs. Kipsang to stay at school during the lunch break so the girls could do my hair in the amazing cornrow braids.

"Oww! Could you not pull so hard?" It felt like Tabitha was ripping my hair out.

"It is the only way to get the braids tight," Nina said. "It looks nice. Would you like to see?"

I needed proof that my head wasn't bleeding, so I said yes. The girls walked me over to the reflective window and I stared at my new hairdo.

"I have a big face."

"It only appears that way, since your hair is not ... um ..." Faith put her hand to her mouth.

"What, sticking out all over the place? It's been tough, you know, to look decent without electricity to use my blow dryer and straightener." I rubbed my hands over the bumpy braids all over my head. "This would be the perfect hairdo for softball games."

"It is the perfect hairdo for just about anything," Nina said.

I couldn't wait to see what people back at the village had to say about it.

Chapter 28

Y ou look like us now," Masara said, when I saw her that night.

I grinned and handed her a big plate of chicken that I had helped Akeelah prepare for the children. "I didn't kill or pluck this, in case you were wondering."

She laughed, "This looks delicious, Riley. Would you like to stay and eat with us?"

I looked at Faith, and she shrugged. "Is there room?"

Masara grinned, "There is always room."

Fawn, Faith, Grace, Hope, and I all came for dinner and squeezed into a room with all twenty-four of Masara's kids. Johanna prayed while we all held hands in a circle:

"Dear Jesus, thank you for all the chicken, and ugali and vegetables. Thank you for friends and for Masara and for clean clothes. And thank you for Riley coming to visit. And, Jesus, thank you for ... um ... let me think ... oh yes. Thank you for you! Amen."

I looked over and saw that Fawn was a little teary-eyed, but I didn't blame her. I had never felt so welcomed by a group of people that hardly knew me. This was an awesome family!

After we finished dinner, we played with the kids for

a while. Then we headed back to our hut. Even though it was the weekend and there was no school the next day, Faith wanted to study anyway.

Mom met me at the front door and handed me a package. "Kiano took me into the city today. This came for you."

I stared at the package. It was addressed to me and it looked like my brother's writing. "Any news about Eric and Drew yet? They've been looking for them forever."

"We're getting close," Mom said. "We'll be going home soon."

I traced my name on the package. "I miss Dad and Brady."

"Me too," Mom said. She gave me a hug. "Enjoy your package. I loved what was in mine."

Mom went over and lay down on her bed. She looked tired, but happy.

It was getting dark inside the hut, so I pulled out my solar light, sat down on the bed, and tore the package open. I laughed when the first thing to fall out was a chocolate donut.

"What was that, a bouncy ball?" Grace knelt down to pick up the donut that had rolled under the bed. She examined it carefully, then tapped it against the wall. "Hard as a rock," she said.

"Why do you have a donut in your mail?" Faith asked. "Is someone afraid you will starve here in Kenya?"

"No." I felt my face heat up. "There's this guy at home. I've known him ever since I was little. He brings a chocolate donut to me every week at church."

"That is sweet," Grace said. "I could write a story about him. The Donut Prince!" She pulled out her spiral notebook and pen. "What is his name?"

"Sean."

Grace scribbled some words in her notebook. "The son of the king of ... let me see ... Fresnolia. Yes, that sounds good. Prince Sean ... uh, what is his last name, Riley?"

I grimaced. "O'Reilly."

They both giggled.

Grace continued, "Prince Sean O'Reilly wasn't happy doing the things most princes do, like riding grand horses and slaying evil dragons. Instead, Prince Sean loved to bake, so he lived and worked at the donut shop with the commoners. One day, Prince Sean was working in the bakery, and he was up to his elbows in dough. Through the window, he caught a glimpse of the fair lady Riley Mae, who had come in to buy a chocolate donut. Prince Sean noticed her African braids and immediately fell in love and decided to marry her one day. The only problem was that Riley was a world traveler who loved shoes, and she hardly noticed Prince Sean, even though he sent donuts to her wherever she traveled *and* he was the most handsome man in the whole world."

"The *whole* world? Really, Grace?" Faith shook her head and looked at me. "Her imagination runs wild sometimes."

"It is only a pretend story," Grace said. "You will like the ending, Riley. I think that Prince Sean is going to slay a dragon for you."

I laughed, "That sounds interesting. Can you name the dragon Morgan?"

She crinkled up her forehead. "That is not a dragon name. Hmmm. But how about … Morgansithor?"

"I like that."

"Great," Faith said. "So finish the story quietly. Some of us are trying to study."

"Fine," Grace smiled, flipped over on her stomach, and continued writing.

I moved into the eating area of the little hut and finished opening my package. The next thing I pulled out was a little box that was labeled "Danger." Inside the little box was a teensy-weensy plastic alligator. A note was attached:

Hi Riley,

This is Gerald. Soak him in a tub of water for four to seven days.

He will grow to full size and then he can assist you in fighting off wild animals while in Kenya. Also, Dad is ready to discuss the possibility of bringing home a puppy, but he refuses to do so until you return. So … hurry.

Love, Brady

Ha! If only Brady knew how difficult water was to come by over here. But the thought was nice.

I dropped the alligator in a cup of water. Then I opened a pink envelope with TJ's writing on it. A bunch of softball confetti fell out of it.

Hey Riley,

Surprise! Haha! Don't you hate when people put confetti in envelopes? When are you coming home? We need to plan your birthday party! And we have to buy clothes for school! Your dad said you're on another secret photo shoot for the Riley Mae shoes! Well, hurry up and model them already!! We've got serious eighth grade plans to make!

Your Best Friend Who NEVER Sees You Anymore,

TJ

Good old TJ. She never ends a sentence with a period. I missed her goofy drama about every little thing, and I wondered how she would have handled the "real" drama I was experiencing over here in Kenya. She probably wouldn't think a charging rhino was as big a deal as losing a softball game.

I picked up the confetti and stared at the pile of it in my hand. Practicing softball in TJ's backyard and then playing games with her was one of my favorite things to do in the world. She's number 22 and I'm number 8. TJ made me promise in fourth grade that we would never change our numbers or be on different teams as long as we lived. Looking back, I suppose that was a little unrealistic since fourth graders really can't control anything. But remembering that promise now made me really appreciate TJ's loyalty. No matter what, that girl would always be my friend.

And I missed her!

Three more letters were in my little package.

Hi Riley,

How's your broken hand? I hope your cast is off and you are throwing softballs again. I want to thank you for being my friend and for helping me have such a fun vacation in Montana. My mom has been calling me a lot, and she's trying to get a transfer to work at Valley Children's Hospital here in Fresno. Dad still can't forgive her for deserting us. Mom finally explained it—she left to protect me. I guess one day when I was little she passed out after drinking and I was all alone in the house for hours. It scared her. She didn't want me to get hurt, so she left. I sort of understand. But I got hurt anyway, you know? Well, I guess only God can fix this mess. I've been going to church every week, and I never see TJ there. I hope she still believes.

Love, Rusty

Wow. No exclamation points in that letter from Rusty. But that last sentence about TJ caused me to sit up a little straighter.

The next letter was from Dad. I took a deep breath, and my shoulders shook a little:

How's my girl?

That's all it took to make me start to cry. I grabbed a tissue from my pocket and wiped my eyes before anyone noticed.

Dad, your girl is safe. But she's sleeping in a mud hut and she needs a hug from you. And if she ever gets home, she plans to tell you every day how glad she is to have you for a dad.

I folded the letter up and decided to read it later when I wasn't feeling so homesick.

The last letter was in a bright orange envelope. It could only be from Sunday. I could pretty much hear his famous laugh which begins at his toes and travels up to his mouth and pops out to everyone's surprise. I actually expected rays of sunshine to flash out at me as I opened the letter.

Instead, I was shocked to see writing that looked like it had been scrawled with a shaky hand.

HELLO, MY FRIEND,

PLEASE PRAY FOR ME. I DO NOT THINK THE TREATMENTS ARE WORKING THIS TIME. BUT GOD IS GOOD. PLEASE GIVE KENYA A HUG FROM ME.

SUNDAY

I turned the paper over, looking for more, but that was it. And that concerned me. Sunday always had so much more to say. And what was that about giving Kenya a hug? He must have been on meds or something when he wrote the letter. But then, he might have really meant for me to hug the whole country for him. God knows Sunday could do it if he were here.

I could feel the tears coming back and was afraid I was going to lose it. I needed fresh air, fast.

I walked out the door of the hut and down to the circle in the center of the village.

"Okay, Sunday, I'll give it my best shot, just for you."

I looked out through a clearing at what was left of the orange, red, and yellow African sunset. I stared at it for a minute, and then realized what I had wrong in my watercolor painting. I forgot to add the oval-shaped trees with the unique branches that appear as dark shadows in front of all that color. I also left out the tinges of purple created by the long, stretched-out clouds. And, if I watched long enough, I imagined I would eventually see a giraffe's long neck adding its shadow to the landscape.

"This is beautiful," I whispered, and I suddenly wished

that Dad, Brady, TJ, Rusty, and Sunday could all be here with me to enjoy God's amazing creation.

I stretched my hands out as far as they could go. "I love you, Kenya," I said, and then I wrapped my arms around myself, nice and tight. It was the best, most peaceful hug ever.

Then I heard a click, and I practically jumped out of my Sole Fires.

"Hey, squirt, can you do that again? Only this time, hold your arms up a little higher."

"Flip?" I kicked dirt in his direction. "You just about scared me to death! Can't you tell I'm having a moment here?"

Flip stuck out his bottom lip. "Aw, I'm sorry. It's just that I was out here taking sunset pictures, and there you appeared." He clicked the buttons on the back of his camera, and then took it off the tripod and held it out for me to see. "Here. Check it out. I think you got your smile back."

It was an amazing picture.

"This one's going to show up in a magazine, isn't it?"

Flip nodded. "It's a frontrunner, that's for sure. But we've still got a lot of Africa to go."

"Please don't say that."

"What? I thought you were beginning to like it here."

I shrugged, and turned back toward the setting sun. "It's growing on me. I really like the people."

"They like you too." Flip tugged on one of my braids. "And these are a nice touch."

"Are you joking?"

"No, I mean it. You really *are* Mae Kiplabat, aren't you?"

I put my hands on my hips and sighed, "Maybe. I'm starting to tolerate African food, I'm building up some good water-hauling muscles, and I actually feel like a real runner now. Hey! Would you like to race me back to the huts? I'm getting pretty fast. I can run a whole 5K now."

I took off and beat Flip, mostly because of his cast, but also because he had a big camera case and a tripod to drag back with him. I guess I should have helped him with that stuff, but he deserved some punishment for being a sneaky photographer.

I opened the door to the girl hut and then turned to wave good night to Flip.

"Sleep well on the floor," I said.

He smiled. "I love the floor. Hey, don't forget—road trip tomorrow!"

"What? We're going somewhere?"

"Haven't you checked the date? Tomorrow's your birthday safari!"

Chapter 29

"Riley, wake up!"

This time, Grace and Faith shook me into the morning.

"Wait," I put a hand up. "It's Saturday. Don't you guys sleep in *ever*?"

"Why would we want to sleep in on the day of our field trip?" Grace bounced up and down on the bed. "It is going to be so fun, Riley!"

"We're not leaving while it's still dark, are we?"

"No, but we have prayer," Faith said. "And then we will help this morning with the water."

"Okay, let's go." I climbed out from under the mosquito net and grabbed my Bible. I ran my fingers over my nice and neat braids. "For once, I think I'm ready."

We were early to prayer at Akeelah's. Some of the ladies had arrived, but they were chatting in low voices. We started to make our way to our regular piece of wall, but Akeelah stopped us short.

"Riley Mae, I would like for you to stay here in front with me so our group can say a prayer for you today. Is there anything of special concern in your life?"

Oh boy. Where should I start? Do these ladies even know why I'm here?

"She would like to get her cast off. Right, Riley?" Good one, Faith.

"Oh yeah, that. I would also like to still be able to throw a softball when I do get it off."

"It will be good for your hand to be healed." Akeelah smiled. Then she put one hand on her heart, and the other one on my shoulder. "But how are things on the inside?"

Hmm. A deep question. Usually people don't ask me those.

"Uh … I guess I worry about safety for me and my family. And, even though I like all of you, I really want to go home."

Akeelah looked me in the eyes and nodded. "I have been praying that for you already."

"Oh, thanks."

"And God has shown me that he brought you to Kenya in order to serve a very special purpose."

"Really? What?"

By now, Faith and Grace had gone to sit against our favorite wall, leaving me alone to counsel with Akeelah. We sat down on the bench and continued to talk while the other women filed into the hut.

"I do not know, but maybe you do. Have you thought much about it, Riley?"

"A little," I was silent a minute, but then I decided to just let it all out. "I think it has to do with shoes."

Akeelah pointed down at my feet, "The shoes that you are modeling?"

I fidgeted a little on the bench. "No. It has to do with the Good News Shoes. It's something I learned from

Ephesians 6:15, in the Bible. It's about taking the good news of the gospel wherever I go. God won't let me forget about that verse. And I think maybe he brought me here to tell some of the children about Jesus."

"That sounds exactly like something God would want to do."

I fidgeted some more. "But, Akeelah, I'm just a kid. I barely know where to start. I'm afraid that anything I say will sound cheesy."

"Cheesy?" She wrinkled her brow. "I do not know what that means."

"Oh, sorry. It means I don't want to sound weird ... or fake, or—okay—sometimes I don't even think I'll be able to spit out one single word that makes sense."

"Oh." She threw her hands up in the air. "I understand now. You are afraid."

I hung my head. "I guess that's it. It's horrible, huh?"

"No, it is not. We are all afraid to share our faith sometimes. But the Bible says that God has not given us a spirit of fear and timidity, but of power, love, and self-discipline. The apostle Paul wrote that to a young man named Timothy. He was not as young as you, but he needed encouragement to be bold, just like you do. Just like we all do."

I shrugged. "I guess you're right."

"The important thing to remember is this: fear does not come from God. But love does. Riley, all you need to do is ask God to help you really love the person you want to share with, and then just open your mouth. The fear will flee, and the good news will come out."

"But how can I really love *each* person? That could be super hard."

Akeelah nodded. "It is impossible—on your own. Only God can help with that." She smiled. "So *that* is what I will have the women pray for today."

So the women prayed. Not that my hand would be able to throw a softball, or even that I could be home in Fresno by my birthday. Instead, they prayed that I would love people with genuine love, and that when I open my mouth, the good news of Jesus would come out, plain and clear, so that people would hear and be given hope.

Chapter 30

Flip met us outside on our way out of the prayer meeting.

"You guys need to hurry up about the water thing. The matatus will be here pretty soon."

I rubbed my hungry belly. "I hope a matatu is some kind of breakfast item. Possibly a donut?"

Grace laughed.

"A matatu is a bus," Faith said, then turned to Flip. "Is that how we are traveling to the safari?"

"Well, our little Jeeps aren't big enough to carry Masara's kids and us."

"They're *all* going?" I grabbed my water jug.

"All but the little ones. We're taking two matatus to a safari lodge, where we'll begin our adventure." He flashed us one of his big smiles and winked.

"Yay! Maybe I'll finally see some monkeys," I said.

"Yeah, but I'm telling you, they're the kind of adventure you *don't* want," Flip said. "Then, if we survive the night, we'll go to Ruth's Village tomorrow. Now I bet you wouldn't get a birthday party that good in Fresno."

Faith and I joined the parade of women and older girls on the trek to collect water.

"What's Ruth's Village?" I asked Faith.

"It is a children's home about an hour from here. I think maybe fifty or so orphans live there."

"Another group of orphans? How can that be?"

"Disease, crime, poverty," Faith said. "I am a very blessed girl to still have both of my parents. I pray so hard for their health every day." She put her head down. "I guess I should have been praying just as hard for my brother."

I put my hand on Faith's shoulder. "We've all been praying. And Flip will make sure that he gets the best care possible. He's going to be okay."

Faith lifted her head and smiled. "Thank you, Riley. I needed an encouraging word today."

As we hauled the water in to the village circle, we saw two very colorful busses parked with the back doors open. Kids from Masara's houses were bringing out small bags, and Kiano and Jomo packed them in the back of the busses. Some of the boys were kicking around the famous sisal-strand ball.

Fawn ran into the group of boys and managed to get the ball away from them. She kicked it over to the edge of the dirt circle and into a box that was lying on its side. She threw her arms up, "Goal!" The boys all cheered, and she high-fived them. Then she ran over to us. "You better get packed. We're leaving pretty soon."

Faith and I ran into our hut and threw a few things into a small suitcase. We met the whole group out by the matatus in a matter of minutes. Mom had a sack of something she was handing out to all the kids.

"Would you like some mandazi?" Mom held the bag out to me.

"Are these donuts?" I grabbed one, gasped, and took a bite. Yum. "They are!" I grabbed another. "Where'd these come from?"

Mom shrugged and gestured to Flip. "Somewhere in the city of Eldoret. He said he wanted to start your birthday weekend out right."

I ran over and gave Flip a hug.

"What was that for? You usually punch me."

"Yeah, I know. And you usually deserve it. But not today. Thanks for the donuts."

"Oh, is that what all this sappy huggy stuff is all about? Well, just wait. Things are about to get even better." He wiggled his eyebrows up and down a few times.

For some reason that made me nervous. "What are you talking about?"

Flip stomped his foot with the ankle cast on the ground. "I don't know about you, Shoe girl, but this cast is cramping my style. I can't go on a safari with this."

I reached down and pulled my cast away from my arm a little. I stared down into it and scrunched my nose. "I know what you mean. And I'm sort of afraid that my skin is rotting under there."

Flip tried to reach his nose to his ankle cast, but came up short. "Good thing I can't reach mine." He winked. "What do you say we get rid of these things today?"

I put my cast behind my back. "Oh no, don't tell me. You found your hacksaw."

"Nope, better. I found a doctor!" Flip turned and

limped off toward one of the matatus. "Hey, Doc! I've got a patient for you!"

Of course I wasn't going to just stand there and let Flip mess with me, so I ran after the silly jokester. As I approached the matatu, I ran into a line of Masara's kids.

"What are you guys waiting for?" I asked.

"Doctor Suzanne is here from Eldoret," one of Masara's boys, named Jacob, said with a smile. "She is giving us our checkups and immunizations."

"Riley," Mom called from inside the matatu. "Come in here, please."

I weaved my way past the kids in line and stepped up into the big, colorful bus. Inside were Flip, my mom, and a dark-haired white lady wearing a colorful smock with angels on it. She held what looked like a portable drill, only it had a circular saw thing on the end. She held her left hand out to me.

"Hi, Riley, I'm Doctor Suzanne Richards." She reached out and shook my good hand. "Would you like to have that dirty old cast removed right now?"

My mouth dropped open. "Are you an angel?"

She laughed, "Hardly. But I do have the latest low noise, kid-friendly, battery-operated cast saw from Stanford University."

"That's awesome!" I held up the orangy-brown, mud-blotched, smelly plaster. "I'm ready to dump this thing whenever you are." I turned my head away and pinched my nose.

When she started up the saw I got a little nervous. With the way things were going these days, I wondered if maybe she would make a mistake and cut my arm off or something. But the nervousness turned to joy as soon as I felt real air touch my wrist.

"There you go, Miss Riley," Doctor Suzanne said, as she freed me from my plaster prison. "Your hand may be a different color than the rest of your arm for a while, but it's good as new."

She bent my wrist several ways. It seemed stiff, but it didn't hurt. Then she poked on top of my hand, where I had smashed it on the rock in the river. It felt a little numb.

"It's looking good," she smiled and looked at my mom. "Young bones heal rapidly." She patted me on the shoulder. "I don't think you'll even need a brace."

I twisted my wrist around and even tried my softball snap a couple of times. It felt so good to be free!

"Hey, is it okay if I throw with this thing?"

Mom crossed her arms and gave me a stern look. "Riley ..."

The doctor looked confused. "What do you want to throw?"

"I'm not sure yet."

Doctor Suzanne put her hand to her chin. "I think it'll be okay. The bones are healed. I'd start slowly, though, since you haven't been using those muscles."

I shook my wrist a little and poked the top of my hand again. It felt a little better. "I'll take it easy."

"I doubt that," Mom said.

"It'll be fine," Doctor Suzanne said and reached out her right hand this time to shake mine.

I decided to hug her instead. I buried my head in her angel smock. She smelled like fresh-cut lemons. "Thank you soooo much."

Doctor Suzanne looked like she was tearing up. "You're welcome. This is why I'm here. It was very nice to meet you, Riley. How long are you going to be in Kenya?"

I shrugged and looked at Mom.

"Not too much longer," she said.

"Hey, is it my turn now?" Flip sat in the bench seat at the back of the bus, holding up his ankle cast.

"Oh, yuck," I grabbed mom by the elbow. "We have to get out of here!"

She grinned. "Good idea. Let's go for a walk. I have some good news to share with you."

Chapter 31

I followed Mom out to the dirt circle, and back through all the mud huts. She didn't say a word until we got inside the cornfield. "They caught Drew in Colorado."

I pumped my newly freed fist in the air. "Yes! So why did he want to hurt us? I mean, isn't he Chuck's son? I don't get it."

Mom pulled off a corn plant leaf and started ripping little pieces off and dropping them. She looked into the sky. "The details shouldn't concern you, honey. Just be happy we caught him."

"What do you mean, it shouldn't concern me? I was the one who went down that waterfall because of him." It was my turn to pull off a leaf and rip.

Mom sighed. "Okay, but this is just between you and me."

I stood up a little straighter. "Thank you. I promise not to say anything to anybody."

Mom smiled. "I believe you won't. Yes, Drew is Chuck Edwards' son, and he has a drug problem."

"Oh," I said.

Chuck Edwards was the nicest guy we met in Montana and a long-time family friend of Flip and Fawn.

"I'm sorry to hear that. But what does that have to do with us and Swiftriver?"

"Well, it doesn't, really, except that people with drug problems need money to support their habit, so sometimes they're willing to do things for money that other people would never do."

I just stared at Mom.

"In this case," Mom continued, "Drew was willing to drop a backpack on Flip at the top of Half Dome, tamper with landing gear on the Swiftriver jet ..."

"And knock Matt out of a raft with a volleyball net?" I looked at Mom with wide eyes and I ripped my leaf some more.

"Yes. According to Drew, it was to scare Flip and Fawn into closing Swiftriver," Mom said.

"That's horrible!" I said. "Why would anyone want Swiftriver to close?"

"Revenge, I guess. You have to remember, Flip and Fawn made a lot of enemies when they testified against the people who killed their father."

"So, who paid Drew to do all those things?" Then I gasped, "Was it Eric?"

"Drew says no," Mom said. "But he won't say who it was."

"Was Eric holding the other end of the volleyball net?" I remembered seeing the pictures Flip took of our doomed rafting trip. He had captured a clear picture of Drew, but he wasn't focused on the other side of the river, so we never knew who helped him.

Mom put her hand up. "No. Drew says he acted alone.

Apparently, he tied the other end of the net to a tree. He claims Eric had nothing to do with anything."

"But then, why would Eric run away from the ranch after the raft accident?"

Mom shook her head. "Maybe he didn't."

Chapter 32

It felt like a school field trip on the matatus with the sixteen kids from the village. We laughed and sang and played games during the bumpy ride. I had so much fun that I barely looked out the windows to see where we were going. We stopped at one point so we could all get some fresh air and go to the bathroom out in nature. We also had some packaged lunches with sandwiches, fruit, and bottled water.

Finally, we arrived in the Masai Mara National Reserve, which Kiano called "the greatest animal show on earth." As we pulled up to the modern-looking safari lodge, the kids in my matatu all cheered.

"Are you ready to see the 'Big Five'?" Jomo asked.

"Hmmm." I scratched my head and looked out at the never-ending grasslands all around us. "Lemme guess what they are. Elephant, lion, hippo, giraffe, and rhino?"

Faith shook her head, "Close. The list includes elephant, lion, leopard, buffalo, and rhino."

"How come a giraffe isn't considered big?"

"Oh, a giraffe is big, but very gentle. The big five are called that because they are the most dangerous."

"So, we're going out there to see them … up close?"

"We will be fine," Faith said. "I have done this many times. The safari guides are experienced and the vehicles we ride in are safe."

"Okay. Because I really do want to live longer than thirteen years, you know."

"I will make sure of that," Jomo said.

Flip lugged over his ever-present camera bag. "I just hope we don't have to run for our lives today. My ankle still feels a little funny."

"Well, you're not supposed to run anyway." I waved my finger at Flip. "Only food runs."

Several open-topped Jeep-like things came rolling up toward the matatus. The guy who was driving the first one jumped out and gathered us around.

"We must get going now, so please put your gear in the lodge lobby and we will check you into your rooms later."

We all did what we were told, then separated into smaller groups, and climbed into the Jeeps. Ours had ten seats in it, but of course, Flip sat right next to me.

"You better behave," I said.

Faith, Grace, Kiano, Jomo, Mom, and Fawn all climbed in the Jeep.

"Awww," I sighed. "We're all together for this one!"

Grace frowned. "Hope was so sad she could not come."

"Oh, no! We're a doomed safari," Flip said as he clicked our picture. "We have no HOPE!" He elbowed me in the ribs. "Get it? No hope?" He chuckled at his own joke.

Our driver, a thin smiling guy named Sironka, jumped in and started up the Jeep. He revved the engine a little and then stood and turned around to talk to us. I liked his British accent.

"I am happy to be your tour guide today on our safari. In the Masai Mara National Reserve we see many beautiful animals. This is where they live, it is not a zoo. They can do whatever they want to do, and they can go anywhere they want to go. And they may have predators in hot pursuit! So, it is my job to make sure that you have a fun and safe day viewing the animals."

"We'll do anything you say," I said.

Sironka gave me a high five. "Very good. The most important thing is to stay in the vehicle at all times, unless I say it is okay to get out. In addition to that, please keep your arms and legs inside, do not stand up, and do not wave things around. The animals can become very agitated by that. Also, if we come close to an animal, you must stay quiet. If an animal becomes hostile, I will do my best to get us out of the way."

"I want to see some monkeys," I said.

Sironka shook his head. "Monkeys can be bad news, so watch out."

"A monkey peed on me once," Grace said.

Sironka smiled and pointed at Grace. "Yes, that is exactly what they like to do."

Then he looked back and waved to the drivers of the two Jeeps behind us. And off we went!

Chapter 33

I t didn't take long at all to see wild animals.

"Wildebeest are migrating," Sironka pointed to the back of a large pack. "That is what they do for their whole life."

"I always thought a wildebeest was a made-up animal," I said.

"They are very real," Sironka said. "In a month or so, you can see thousands more out here."

They looked funny, but big—too big to imagine a group of a thousand of them running around.

"Why do they have to keep on migrating? Can't they just find a home and stay put?"

"They must find food, and they must keep from becoming food." Sironka sped the Jeep up a hill and stopped at the top. He pointed to some spotted animals a hundred feet or so off the side of the road. "That wildebeest didn't quite make it."

One of the leopards turned toward us. He stood and then circled around his lunch.

"Poor thing," I said.

"The leopards have to eat too," Faith said.

Sironka drove down the hill and in a matter of

minutes I began to feel like I was at the Wild Animal Park in San Diego.

"This is so beautiful!" Mom took pictures with her phone. "I can't wait to send these to Dad and Brady."

A wave of sadness came over me as I thought again of the reason I was here. In fact, I guess I felt a little like a wildebeest, moving from place to place trying to avoid danger all the time.

The other Jeeps were right behind us. One of the boys roared like a lion. The guide shushed him.

Sironka stopped the Jeep at one point and told us we could get out and stand in an area behind some thick bushes. "We can see lions from here without being seen. You must be very quiet though."

I was a little scared, so I stayed close to Mom as we watched a lioness play with some cute little cubs. They looked harmless enough, almost like you could walk up and start wrestling with them.

"There," Faith said. "You've wanted to see lions. Be glad we never saw any on our way to school."

The whole safari was breathtaking, and as the day went on I was filled with awe by the beauty of the wide-open playground for some of God's most interesting creations.

"I want to feed the giraffes," Grace said.

Kiano shook his head. "They are capable of getting their own food out here."

"God sure was creative when he made those," I said.

"He was just getting started with the animals," Kiano said. "Think about how beautiful and complex people are. Not one is the same."

* * *

After taking a little snack break behind another big bush, we jumped back in the Jeep. Sironka turned the key, but the engine sputtered and died. He tried the key a few more times, but nothing happened.

"Ha! Are we out of gas?" Flip snapped a few pictures of Sironka struggling with the key.

Sironka jumped out of the Jeep and popped the hood. He studied the engine compartment for minute, and then he got back in and turned the key. This time the engine sputtered, but at least it started. He looked back at all of us and grinned. "That has never happened before. This is the new Jeep."

Fawn looked around at the inside of the Jeep. "Are you sure this is the new one? It's got a million dents on the outside, and the upholstery looks a little faded."

"That is what happens on safari," Jomo said. Then he turned to Sironka. "Would you like for me to look? I know a little about vehicles."

Sironka brushed him off. "Oh, no. The safari is coming to an end, so when we return I will have our mechanic look at it."

"Wait," Faith said. "We cannot be finished yet. We have not seen all of the big five."

I counted on my hand. "Let me see. Lion, rhinos, buffalo, leopard …" I scanned the horizon, saw a few more wildebeests and giraffes, but I knew they didn't qualify. And then I heard something rustling through the grass on the right side of the road.

Something very big.

Chapter 34

The rustling turned to crunching as a family of elephants crossed in front of our Jeep and then stopped on the roadway. First a big one, then a couple of cute small ones like Muna at the elephant orphanage. The kids in the Jeeps behind us gasped and pointed, and I heard the guide shush the same kid who this time made a trumpet noise with his mouth. Sironka simply held one hand up while turning the engine off with the other.

Fawn elbowed me and pointed to another group of elephants coming up behind our Jeep on the roadway. "We're surrounded," she whispered.

I suddenly felt claustrophobic and wanted to escape. I'd never heard of an elephant eating a person, but I did remember a story that a speaker told at camp once about a zookeeper that almost got sat on by an elephant. It was supposed to be a hilarious story, but now that I was so close to the huge beasts I could see the story from the zookeeper's viewpoint, and I wasn't amused anymore.

The elephants stayed standing just a few feet in front of our Jeep. They turned and looked behind us, like they were waiting for the other elephants to catch up.

"Should we back up and get out of here?" I asked Sironka.

He just shook his head and held his hand up again.

Flip clicked picture after picture. "This is so cool," he whispered. "Man, Riley, I wish there was a way I could get a picture of you with one of them."

"Don't hold your breath," I whispered back. "I'm not moving."

Right then, we heard some loud snorting, and Sironka stood up, turned around and looked over my head, his eyes wide. Mom and Fawn turned too, and their eyes did the same thing.

"The bull," Sironka said.

Flip turned his camera toward the back of the Jeep. "Don't ... move ... Riley. Looks like I may get my wish." He aimed his camera at my face, clicked it, and then he showed me the digital image.

The picture was of me with a terrified look on my face in front of a huge elephant with long tusks standing right behind our Jeep. His ears were spread out wide on each side of his head.

"He looks mad," I whispered, barely moving my lips.

The two Jeeps behind us started up their engines and roared off in reverse. I turned in time to see the elephant running at them, but then it stopped.

"Hold on," Sironka said.

Then he turned the key on our Jeep. The engine sputtered a little and then died. He tried again, but the only noise came from the elephant behind us, who was now turned back in our direction and didn't look happy at all.

"We are in between him and his family, so we appear to be a threat. I will try to scare him off." Sironka left his driver's seat, came around, and jumped onto the back fender of the Jeep. He began pounding on the back bumper with a rock. No wonder there were dents.

"Go on now, get out of here!" Sironka waved his arms in the air.

The elephant moved closer and snorted some more. Sironka pounded harder.

I actually felt the air on the back of my neck from the next snort. I didn't dare move my head. Flip clicked and clicked.

Jomo had moved to the driver's seat and was trying to start the Jeep. But the engine wouldn't turn over. I watched as the group of elephants in front of us moved to the other side of the road and walked off into the high grasses.

"Go with your family! Go away!" Sironka continued to pound the rock with one hand and wave at the elephant with the other.

"He's backing up a little," Flip whispered, while he was still clicking.

"His ears are still out," Sironka said. "He is preparing to charge. You all must get out and run right now."

"RUN?" I almost shouted. "But I thought we're NEVER—"

"NOW!" Sironka yelled, and a bunch of hands grabbed me. Somehow, I ended up in front of the Jeep, and then all of us—except Flip and Sironka—ran away from the Jeep and toward a tree. And I *almost* ran as fast as Faith!

Lord, please help Sironka! I prayed. *And help us! Please don't let there be lions out here!*

Who was I kidding? I had just witnessed that the place was full of lions.

Jomo grabbed my hand and pulled me between himself and the tree. We all turned and watched as the elephant charged the Jeep. Sironka managed to jump back to the front seat, but was still facing the elephant and yelling. Flip disappeared. It looked like he had scrunched down to the floor of the Jeep. We watched in horror as the furious elephant lifted the back end up and pushed it several feet. Sironka was ejected over the front and onto the dirt.

"Oh no! He's going to get run over!" I pointed and jolted forward, but Jomo held me back.

Sironka managed to get up and out of the road just as the elephant pushed the Jeep a few feet farther.

He reached our group by the tree and brushed the dirt off his pants. "The elephant will stop in a minute if the man with the camera holds still."

We watched as the massive beast pushed, then stopped. Pushed, then stopped. Then he looked in our direction, raised his trunk in the air, and let out a deafening trumpet sound.

"What should we do?" Mom asked, as she fiddled around in her safari vest. I wondered if she had packed some sort of weapon in there.

Sironka cracked a small grin. "Nothing. His temper tantrum is about over."

The bull elephant kicked the Jeep a couple of times more and snorted. Then he just stood still for several seconds.

"Don't move, Flip," I whispered.

The original group of elephants returned to the roadway between the Jeep and the bull. They stared at each other, but didn't move.

"Go," Sironka said quietly. "Go be a happy family now."

Those words must have held some kind of magic, because as soon as Sironka said them, the bull and the other elephants walked into the bushes.

Fawn called Flip's name and ran over to the Jeep.

"Whew," I said. "Now what should we do?"

Mom grabbed hold of my shirt. "You stay right here, missy."

We watched as Fawn climbed into the Jeep.

"Jomo! Can you come here?" Fawn waved him over, but we all went running toward the Jeep.

Soon we were all standing there staring at Flip, who was lying down on the Jeep floor, still holding his camera, with his eyes closed.

Fawn reached down and patted his cheek. "Flip?"

He didn't have a scratch on him. In fact, he looked fine. So why were his eyes closed?

"Oh my," Sironka said. "This does not look good."

Chapter 35

ROOOOOAAAAARRRR!" Flip sat up, wild-eyed. We all jumped back and screamed. Flip, had his camera poised for pictures or a video of the whole thing.

Fawn grabbed her chest, but then she lunged at her brother and shook him.

"Are you KIDDING me? Why would you scare us like that? I'm going to call that elephant back to finish you off for that little stunt!"

Flip laughed, "I'm sorry. I just couldn't help myself. Riley, I can't believe you screamed too. You should know better by now. Man, that trick never gets old." He stood up and turned around. "See? I'm okay. Not even a scratch."

"You're a brat!" I said. "That was terrifying."

"Yeah, maybe. But not everyone has a bull elephant charge their Jeep while on their birthday safari. Wouldn't you say that's better than going bowling or to a boring movie in Fresno?"

I was so shocked that I didn't know what to say. I was beginning to think "boring" would be a welcome feeling these days.

"Okay," Mom said. "So how are we going to get out of here?"

Jomo pushed open the hood and fiddled around for a minute. Then his head popped out and he smiled and brushed his hands together. "You had a few things loose. Try it now."

Sironka jumped back in the driver's seat and turned the key. The engine rumbled to life this time. He slammed a fist on the dashboard and grinned. "I told you, this is the new Jeep."

We buckled ourselves back in our seats and Sironka drove us to the safari lodge. The kids and other adults had already begun the check-in process in the lobby. When we told them that the bull elephant had charged our Jeep, they acted like it was no big deal. Some of the guides made jokes about how we should have to pay more money for that special entertainment. Flip gave Sironka a huge tip. And the kid who kept getting in trouble made his elephant trumpet noise and said that he wished it had happened to them.

People were definitely different here in Kenya.

* * *

That night, while I lay in bed thanking God that I didn't get crushed by an elephant, and while Faith studied history, Grace continued writing her story about Prince Sean, the donut maker.

"Maybe, after Riley and Prince Sean get married in the story, they could ride off into the sunset on a bull elephant!"

Faith looked up from her book and smiled, "Ooh. I like that ending."

Chapter 36

The next morning, we slept in past five o'clock for a change! I enjoyed sleeping on a nice cushy mattress all by myself. After a late breakfast of mandazi and passion fruit juice, the lodge staff helped us bring our luggage out and load it up. Then, we boarded the matatus again and drove for a couple of hours to Ruth's Village.

As we pulled up to the cluster of new-looking stone buildings, a group of young people—mostly mzungus— were standing by a white van taking pictures with some African children by the front entrance. I watched through the dust-covered window as a man with blondish wispy hair coming out of the bottom of a back-ward ball cap snapped the last picture of the group. Then he jogged off. I never saw his face, but goosebumps rose up on my arms. Nah. It couldn't be.

"Looks like we just missed another missions team," Flip said. "I wonder where they were from."

He limped a little going down the steps of the matatu, and we followed. As the last person piled out, we watched the van with the other team take off down the dirt road.

A tall woman with light-brown curly long hair turned around after waving good-bye to the van. "It's like a revolving door today, but that's okay. We don't usually get this many visitors! I'm Wendi Reynolds. The kids around here call me Aunt Wendi." She looked around. "My husband Jonathan is around here someplace."

"Huh. I thought your name would be Ruth," I pointed to the sign at the front of the children's home.

Wendi nodded. "Ruth is my mom's name, but we picked that name for our home because of the character of Ruth in the Bible. The name Ruth means "friend," or "companion." My husband and I moved to Kenya from the United States because so many kids here need someone who will stick with them like Ruth stuck with Naomi."

"Wow. That seems like it would be hard," I said.

"Nothing worthwhile is ever easy. And it's difficult to explain, but we actually love it here and feel like this is our home now. It's always nice to visit the states though. And to entertain visitors like you."

Wendi looked around again and put her hands on her hips. "My husband has disappeared! He's been working on a special project for your arrival." Wendi addressed the group. "Since we just had a group leave, the staff needs a couple of hours to clean the guest quarters. So for now, why don't you leave your gear on the buses and come out to the courtyard and meet our kids?"

Ruth's Village was home to about fifty children, newborn to age thirteen. I think they were all in the courtyard playing when we got there, even the babies.

The kids from our village all spread out and began playing like they had been here before. Jomo jumped up and sat on the brick wall that surrounded the courtyard while the rest of the grown-ups took off with Wendi somewhere. I just stood and looked around. The kids seemed content to keep playing their games while I watched. Finally, after several minutes, one boy did come running over.

"Hey! You're a kid, like us!" he said. "Usually just grown-ups come. My name is Paul."

"Hi, Paul. I'm Riley Mae."

Paul looked down at my feet. "Nice shoes." He put his fist to his chin. "How old are you?"

"I'm twelve. No—wait a minute—tomorrow's my birthday, so ..."

"You are twelve," Paul said, and then flashed a huge grin.

I laughed, "Yes, I guess you're right. Until tomorrow."

Some kids who were playing basketball called over, "Paul, are you in the game or not?" Paul jerked his head around to them, and then back to me. "Do you play sports?"

"Yes, I do!"

"Then would you like to join our game? My team is not very good. You could help us."

I rubbed the back of my hand and frowned. "I just got a cast off my hand. Maybe I better pass this time."

"Too bad for us," Paul said, and then he looked back and watched a young man throw a basketball up and only hit air. He shook his head. "I better go. I am the only one who can make a basket."

"Yes, it looks like you better hurry."

Chapter 36

"See you after the game, Riley Mae," Paul waved and jogged back over to the court, where he was immediately handed the ball. He dribbled inbounds and then took a shot from the outside line. The ball went in the basket, hitting nothing but net. He looked over at me and smiled.

I gave him a thumbs-up with my new "out of the cast" thumb.

I joined Jomo on the wall to watch the game for a few minutes. Paul was right, his team wasn't very good. But they all looked so happy. In fact, all the kids in the courtyard were having fun. Well, except one. There was one girl who looked to be about my age who was sitting on a bench with her head down. A kind-looking African woman wearing a bright multi-colored dress sat next to her with her arm around her.

I felt a knot form in my throat.

"Riley!" Mom yelled at me from across the courtyard. "Come here! I want to show you something."

I glanced over to the basketball court one more time and watched as Paul made another three-pointer. Then I ran over to where Mom was. Jomo followed. Mom led me out a gate from the courtyard and through an area of dark dirt that looked like it had just been planted with some kind of crop. We walked toward a muscular, brown-haired man sitting on a tractor. Hooked behind the tractor was a chain-link net. The man waved. "Hey. You must be Riley."

I smiled. "Yep, that's me."

The man climbed down from his tractor, pulled off

his work gloves, and held out his hand. "I'm Jonathan Reynolds."

I was thrilled to shake it with my new hand. "Oh, hi. We met your wife earlier. She's really nice."

"Yeah, I kinda like her. Except lately she's been making me work way too much. But at least this last project has been fun. Wanna see?"

"Sure." I followed Jonathan and Mom down the path over a little hill. The adults were there. And a sight I hadn't seen for a long time.

It was a softball field.

Chapter 37

It wasn't as fancy as any of the fields I play on in Fresno. But the dirt infield was flat, and it was groomed—like it had been scraped down with that chain-link thing behind Jonathan's tractor. Real bases were secured into the ground, and chalk lines were drawn to outline the batter's box and the pitcher's circle. The outfield was actual green grass, but not the perfectly groomed stuff we have back home. It was more like the wild stuff that I had seen on our road trips here in Kenya, only mowed short. The mysterious trailer that we'd been pulling all the way from Nairobi was parked on the side of the field.

"What do you think?" Mom asked.

"It's ... awesome."

"Surprise!" Flip jogged up the path. "Man, I thought you'd find out about this, but it turns out you aren't as sneaky as I thought you were."

"Sneaky? Who are you calling sneaky?" I pushed him in the chest when he ran up next to me.

"Well, let's see," he counted on his fingers. "You've invaded my office and my room and my computer ..."

"It's exactly what Nancy Drew would do under the same circumstances. She would call it 'sleuthing.'"

"Okay then. I stand corrected. You aren't as 'sleuthy' as I thought. Therefore, we were able to pull off this surprise for you."

"Isn't it great, Riley?" Fawn asked.

"Um, yeah. I love the field. But why is it a surprise for me?"

"Because," Fawn said, "it's going to be the location of Swiftriver's very first Riley Mae Sports Camp and Shoe Giveaway."

I put my hand on my hip. "Hey, wait a minute … is that in the contract?"

"Dude," Flip said. "Africa isn't in the contract. Riding down waterfalls without a raft isn't in the contract. Fighting off bears in boxes isn't …"

I held my hand up. "Okay, I get it. It actually sounds fun. When do we start?"

"Tomorrow," Fawn said.

"Happy birthday," Mom hugged me and lifted me off the ground.

"Hey, so do I finally get to see what's in the trailer? I'm guessing shoes, since we're having a shoe giveaway?"

"There are a few more things too," Flip said. "Let's go check it out!"

The trailer was filled with shoes all right. Boxes and boxes of Riley Mae shoes. And a few boxes of Swiftriver boy's shoes. Yeah, I guess the boys wouldn't want the girly styles. I smiled as I remembered my friend Sunday, who insisted on wearing the Riley Mae Sole Fire running shoes, because he loves the color orange.

The other side of the trailer had hooks with softball

equipment bags hanging on them. I jumped in, pulled one down, and unzipped it. Inside was a bat, a glove, a batting helmet, visor, jersey, and some cute little hair ties.

A bigger equipment bag sat in the back of the trailer. It contained two sets of catcher's gear, a ton of softballs, and more bats.

"Did we forget something?" Flip scratched his head. "You look confused."

It was then I realized that my mouth was hanging open.

I sat down in the middle of all the stuff in the trailer. I took out one of the gloves, held it to my nose, closed my eyes, and gave it a huge whiff. I felt like I was at home.

"Where'd you guys get all this stuff?" I asked.

Fawn shrugged. "Sporting goods store."

"But, WHEN? I mean, after the raft accident we were at the hospital, and then on the run to Missoula, and then to the hospital to see Sunday ..."

"We always have plenty of time to kill while we wait for you to pack all your girl junk." Flip winked.

"Ha! Most of that junk is shoes, which I got from you."

I took a catcher's helmet out of one of the bags and popped it on my head. "These are top of the line! Are we leaving it all here?"

"Of course," Fawn said. "I'm sure after you teach these kids how to play softball, it's going to be one of their favorite sports."

"I'M going to teach them?"

"Well, it is called the 'Riley Mae' Sports Camp!"

"And everyone gets shoes too?"

"Yes," Fawn said. "It was our goal from the beginning to use the proceeds from the Riley Mae collection to give away free Riley Mae shoes to kids who need them."

"So THAT'S why they're so expensive?"

"That, and each one is kind of a work of art," Fawn said. "This Riley Mae girl is quite unique. Not just any dull-looking shoe will have her signature with the daisy on it."

I laughed at that, "If you say so. I'm just glad these kids are going to get some."

I buried my face in the glove and took another whiff.

I smiled. I guess the best things *aren't* always in the contract.

Chapter 38

"Riley, wake up!"

Grace shook me and I sat straight up, expecting to be under a mosquito net. But instead I was in my own cushy guest bed at Ruth's Village. *Ahhh.*

And it was my thirteenth birthday! I had been waiting all my life for this day! I jumped out of bed, ran into the bathroom, and flicked the light switch. I stared at my face in the mirror. Grace came in after me.

"Huh," I said. "This isn't exactly how I thought I would look when I turned thirteen."

"It's the hair." She pointed to my tight braids that were still hanging in there.

"Maybe. Plus, I kind of thought I would see Fresno in the background." I turned to face Grace.

Grace laughed. "I hope I can visit you in Fresno someday. I will bring you my finished story of Prince Sean and the fair maiden, Riley Mae."

"I would like that! Maybe you can even meet the Prince … er, Sean I mean, for yourself."

Faith joined us in the bathroom. She stared up at the light, took a deep breath, and let it out.

"Electricity is one of my favorite things." Faith headed

over to the sink and turned on the water. She cupped her hands, and let them fill up. Then she splashed it on her face.

"I also love running water."

"Yeah," I said. "It sure beats running *for* water."

Grace splashed a little water on her face too. "I wonder what they are serving for breakfast this morning."

Faith grabbed her sister's hand. "I am pretty sure it is not ugali. Shall we go find out?"

When the three of us entered the dining hall, a bunch of the Ruth's Village kids clapped their hands. The boy named Paul came over and pointed to a cake that was in the middle of one of the tables. It said "Happy Birthday Riley," and under my name, written in fudge frosting, was the number thirteen.

"Congratulations!" He smiled. "You are no longer twelve."

In walked the kids from Faith and Grace's village along with all the adults in our traveling group. They began to sing "Happy Birthday," and all the kids from Ruth's Village joined in with them.

I thought about what I had imagined this day would be like. This wasn't it. But for some reason I was excited anyway. In fact, at that moment, I couldn't think of anything else I'd rather be doing.

And we had pancakes for breakfast! It was the first food I had eaten in a while that seemed like it was from Fresno.

"So Riley," Kiano said, as he took a knife and cut his

huge stack into bite-sized, pie-shaped pieces. "Are you ready to teach this group of kids how to play softball?"

A surge of excitement went through me. "Yes, I am!"

"When we are finished playing, can we come in and eat the cake?" Grace has a definite sweet tooth.

"What?" I said. "Aren't we going to eat it now?"

"It is your birthday," Kiano said. "You may do what you want to do."

We ate the cake before we went out to play.

Chapter 39

Teaching the kids to play softball was fun. Most of them were used to hitting rocks with sticks so almost all of them were able to hit the ball on their first try. Paul was even able to hit over everyone's heads. Getting used to the gloves was a little harder, but after a few drills of fielding grounders and catching flies, they began to get the hang of it.

One thing they loved to do was run the bases. And they were fast. The hard part was getting them to stop running when they got to the base!

"You can only run through first base and home plate. At second and third, you have to stop or someone with the ball can tag you out." I held the ball in my glove and made a sweeping tagging motion toward second base.

"We cannot stop," Faith said. "We are leaning forward and going too fast."

"Then I guess I'll have to teach you how to slide."

So we did sliding drills. I taught them to fold one leg under and to reach out for the base with their extended foot. It was hilarious. Some of them threw their legs up in the air and landed on their backsides, going nowhere. Others couldn't get their legs out in front of themselves, so they kind of tripped and rolled. Most of them started sliding too late and still overshot the base.

This clearly wasn't working. "Okay. Who cares about outs? We'll just give everyone on each team a chance to hit and then we'll switch places."

The kids all cheered.

We formed two teams, the Lions and the Zebras. And we took turns hitting and fielding and running too far and sliding too soon and laughing harder than I had in a long time.

Soon a pickup truck arrived, with Jonathan Reynolds driving.

"This must be our lunch," Wendi said, and she called all the kids over to the truck.

She handed out bags filled with peanut butter and jelly sandwiches, apples, and cookies. Two five-gallon jugs of lemonade helped us wash the yummy food down.

"You kids are dirty!" Wendi said to the crowd as we finished up lunch. "We can't give you new shoes until you change into something more appropriate. Meet us all back in the courtyard in thirty minutes. Make sure you change into clean socks at least!"

The kids gathered up their trash and ran up the hill toward the dorms.

"I'll pull the trailer with the shoes up to the court-yard," Jonathan said.

"Great." Wendi turned to me. "So how do you want to handle the giveaway, Riley?"

I looked around for my "advisors," but the only one

around was Jomo. "You have any idea how to do this, Jomo?"

He shrugged. "I do not know. But I do know that you are a smart girl, so you will figure it out."

"Awww, thanks! I have to admit, I've felt like a dummy ever since I got to Africa."

"Why is that?" Wendi asked.

"Everything is so different. The food, the scenery, the living arrangements. I might as well have gone to another planet."

"I am glad you came here instead," Jomo said. "God has a plan for you."

Wendi smiled, "Hmmm. Sounds like something Jonathan said to me right before we decided to move to Kenya."

Chapter 40

The kids made it back to the dorms, changed, and arrived at the courtyard in roughly ten minutes, which gave me no time to figure out how to give away fifty pairs of shoes.

Wendi saved the day. She had the kids sit in circles according to their ages. Then she led them in some songs and a couple of games while the other adults stacked shoes according to sizes along the brick wall that lined the courtyard. After we finished that, she assigned an adult to each circle, and she told the kids to be patient while that adult got shoes for each one in their group.

My job was to go around and ooh and ahh with the kids over their new shoes. I watched as one little girl traced my name that was written on the tongue with her finger. "I like the daisy," she said. Another girl ran up and hugged me. "Thanks for the shoes!"

Huge smiles covered the faces of all the kids in the yard. Except one. That same girl I saw earlier with the adult worker was again sitting on the bench, this time alone, not a part of any circle.

I had to find out what was wrong. I breathed in deep and walked over the bench. As I approached, the girl looked up.

"Hi," I said, and I waved. "Did you get shoes yet?"

She looked over toward the stacks of shoes on the wall. "No."

"Oh. Well, we need to take care of that. What size do you wear? Oh, and I'm Riley, by the way."

"Yes, I know," she said, and I thought I saw one side of her mouth curl up in a half-smile. "I am Hannah." She looked down at her feet. "I am not sure what size I need. I have been growing a lot lately."

"You too, huh? I know what you mean. All my long pants are turning into capris." I pulled my pants up to expose my ankles and gave her a goofy look, but she didn't respond. Hmm.

"Here ..." I took my shoe off. "Try on mine and we'll go from there."

She took the shoe from me, placed it on the ground and pushed her foot in. I poked my finger on the end of the shoe, to feel for the little space that's supposed to be there, but it wasn't. "Close, but maybe you need a seven."

"I am sorry I do not know," Hannah said. "I have never bought shoes before."

Lord, things just aren't fair!

"That's okay, Hannah. What's your favorite color?"

"Pink."

"Really? That's my favorite color too. Hey, wait here. I might have the perfect pair for you!"

I ran over to the shoes on the wall, praying there would be pink running shoes in a size seven. I almost ran into Fawn as she was turning with a stack of shoe boxes.

"Whoa, not so fast. You're going to flatten someone."

I helped her steady her stack, which almost came up to her eyes.

"Got any sevens in the Pink Flash?"

"Oh, brother. Hang on, I'll set these down and look."

Sure enough, a Pink Flash in a size seven was in the middle of her stack.

"Yes! Maybe these will cheer Hannah up."

Fawn shielded the sun from her eyes as she looked in Hannah's direction.

"Why, what's going on with her?"

I shrugged. "Not sure, really. We just met. She just seems super sad."

"Well, I don't know any girl who doesn't feel a little better when she gets a new pair of shoes."

"Yeah," I giggled. "That's what I was thinking."

As I started making my way over to Hannah, I saw one of the house moms go over and talk to her for a minute, and then give her a hug. A few tears streamed from Hannah's cheeks. This didn't look like something that Riley Mae shoes could fix.

Riley, she needs the Good News Shoes.

I stopped in my tracks. There was that deep whisper voice again! It surprised me, just like it did when I was back at the prayer meeting at Akeelah's house. And this time, even though there was the noise of children playing all around me, I heard it as clear as anything. And I knew I had to obey.

Lord, I don't know what to say.

And then I remembered what Akeelah said: "Love the person, and then open your mouth."

Okay.

I walked over to Hannah and handed her the box of shoes.

"It's your lucky day. Pink Flash, size seven."

She wiped a tear, opened the box, put a hand to her mouth and just stared at the shoes.

I sat down next to her on the bench. I didn't say anything for a minute.

She squeaked out a very quiet "thank you."

I thought about what might be wrong in this young girl's life at the moment. Well, one big thing was obvious. She either didn't have parents, or they couldn't take care of her for some reason—that's why she would be here at Ruth's Village in the first place. I was filled with sadness and as I watched her finally take the shoes out of the box and tie them on her feet, I could honestly say that I felt love for this girl.

It was time to open my mouth.

"Hannah, I'm sorry you're sad. Is there anything I can do to help?"

She looked at me with wide eyes, then down at the ground. "No. There is nothing anyone can do."

"Really? Because there are lots of people around here who might be able to do something. I'm just a kid, but I could talk to them and get you anything you need. Especially shoes."

One side of Hannah's mouth curled up in a grin for a second and then she looked me in the eyes. "I would like to see my mother again. But she died a month ago. I am afraid there is no hope for me."

"I see." A lump formed in my throat and I had to swallow hard to get my next words out. "So there is nothing any human being can do."

"That is right." Hannah lifted her feet up to look at her new Pink Flash feet.

"Hannah, do you know who Jesus is?"

Hannah shrugged. "We have been singing about him here at Ruth's Village. We also pray to him each day. But I do not know who he is exactly."

Right then, Fawn came over and plopped herself down on the stone fence just a few feet away from Hannah and me on the bench. That made me more nervous. But I opened my mouth anyway and this is what came out:

"Hannah, Jesus is God's Son. He came to earth many years ago. While he was here, he healed people of diseases and told everyone about heaven and about what God is like. He loved people, no matter who they were or where they came from or what they had done in their lives. He especially loved kids ..."

I stopped a minute to think, and I watched as the children of Ruth's Village ran around and played in their new shoes. A few of them were bouncing Ping-Pong balls into their old shoes and it looked like they had made it into some kind of game. I could almost imagine Jesus playing with them and having a good time.

"But that's not the main reason he came. You see ... Jesus died on a cross for our sins."

"He died?" Another tear dropped from Hannah's eye. "That is horrible."

"Yeah, it was bad. But it was good for us that he did. Do you know what sin is, Hannah?"

Hannah nodded. "It is when the darkness in our heart comes out."

I thought about that for a second.

"Hey, that's a good answer."

Hannah smiled.

"But it's not quite right. Sin is the darkness that is there, even if we can somehow keep it in."

"It is so hard sometimes."

"Oh, believe me, I know." I put my hand on Hannah's shoulder.

And all of a sudden, I knew where to go with this.

"And that's just it! No matter how hard we try, we can't get rid of that darkness on our own. That's where Jesus comes in. He was perfect—with no darkness in his heart at all. So he died—for us—in our place."

A tear dropped from Hannah's cheek. "That is too sad."

"I know, but it's not the end of the story."

Hannah sniffed and lifted her head. "How is death not the end?"

"Three days later, Jesus *rose* from the dead. He is alive!"

Hannah's eyes widened. "He is?"

"Yes! He beat the darkness of sin and death and sadness and all that awful stuff. The Bible says, 'For God so loved the world that he gave his one and only Son, that whoever believes in him shall not perish but have eternal life.' "

Hannah sniffed a couple more times and didn't say anything for a minute. She straightened her legs and glanced down at her new Pink Flash shoes. Then she looked up to the sky.

"Jesus cannot bring my mother back to me."

Now tears were forming in my eyes. And though I was looking at Hannah, I could hear a little cough and a muffled sob behind me, which had to be coming from Fawn, who was still sitting on that bench.

God, help me know what to say next!

I opened my mouth again. "That is true. But Jesus promises to never leave you. Ever. He will help your heart to heal, and he'll take the darkness away and fill it with peace."

Hannah's eyes met mine. "Really?"

"Yes. Really. You just have to ask him."

"And you have done this?"

I shook my head. "Yes."

"Will Jesus take away my anger and sadness?"

Oh, man. A tough question. As I thought about what to say next, Fawn came over and crowded between us on the bench.

"I don't know about you," she said to Hannah, "but I'm ready to ask Jesus into my life. I've had anger and sadness in my heart for way too long, from way back when *my* mom died. I'm ready to get rid of it. What do you say, Hannah? Do you want to join me?"

And then a crazy thing happened! Hannah said yes. Fawn grabbed her hand. And they both started to pray to ask Jesus to forgive them and for him to come into their lives and take away their sin and their sadness. While Hannah prayed I imagined all the angels in heaven dancing while she swung her feet with the new Pink Flash shoes. And tears streamed down my cheeks as I thanked God for letting me wear his "Good News Shoes."

Fawn and Hannah had barely said amen, when we were interrupted by Flip, who looked upset.

"They're playing Shoe Bounce!" He pointed to Fawn. "Did you teach them that game?"

"What are you talking about? What game?" Fawn looked confused.

"Don't you remember? We made up that game when we were kids."

"I sort of remember. We played lots of silly games, Flip."

"But where did they come up with *that* name for the game?"

"Is that what we called it? What does it matter? We're kind of in the middle of something here."

"So you didn't teach it to them?"

"No. I told you. I hardly remember it."

"So where did they learn it?"

"Who knows? Why don't you ask them?"

"I'll go ask them," I said.

I ran over and asked super-athlete Paul, and he told me.

"We just learned this game from E-rock. He was here with the team that left right before you came."

"*What* was the guy's name?"

"E-rock. He was so fun."

My mind tried to imagine a guy named E-rock, and I pictured a guy with a tall mohawk who plays electric guitar and sings scream-o music.

"Well?" Flip could hardly wait for me to get back to the

bench. "What did you find out?" Fawn and Hannah were talking away and apparently weren't interested in what I found out.

"They said some guy named E-rock taught it to them. He was on the last missions team."

Flip's hands flew to his head. "What? What did you say his name was?"

"E-rock. I know. Weird," I chuckled. "Kinda like the name Flip is weird."

Flip turned around and grabbed Fawn by the arm. "Sis, did you hear that? E-rock was here!"

Fawn's eyes got big. "What? Are you sure?"

Then Flip and Fawn ran off, leaving Hannah and me staring at each other.

"That was strange, huh?"

Hannah nodded. "Riley, what should I do now? I want to learn more about Jesus."

I scratched my head and thought a minute. "I have something I can give you that will really help. But it's packed in my suitcase."

I looked down at her Pink Flash shoes. "So, for now, do you wanna go try out those new running shoes?"

Hannah smiled. "Sure." She jumped off the bench and started running faster than me, all the way down the path from the courtyard out to the softball field. We had a great time running the bases and playing catch until Jomo, who was watching from the sidelines, called for us to come in for dinner. When we got to the dining hall, there was no sign of Mom or Flip or Fawn anywhere. Thankfully, though, there was pizza!

Chapter 41

My birthday went too fast, and we had to say good-bye to our new friends much too soon. The next morning, we all took pictures in front of the Ruth's Village sign, and I got teary eyed as we wheeled our luggage over to load it into the matatus and the now-empty trailer.

Before I threw my suitcase in, I dug inside it and pulled out my Bible. I traced my finger over the pink letters that spelled Riley Mae on the cover. This was the Bible that the church gave me after I was baptized, and I had highlighted a lot of verses with my pink highlighter during lessons with Mrs. O'Reilly in children's church. I pulled out the little foil bookmark that my brother Brady made me—the one that held my place at Ephesians 6:15: *For shoes, put on the peace that comes from the Good News, so you will be fully prepared.*

I placed the bookmark back in my suitcase and zipped it up. Then I took the Bible with me and set out to find Hannah.

"Here," I said when I found her. "This will help you to get to know Jesus better. My teacher at church—Mrs.

O'Reilly—usually tells people to read the book of John first."

I opened the Bible to the book of John, and I folded the corner down of the first page. "There. Now you will know where to find it."

Hannah took the Bible from me and hugged it to her chest. Then she pulled it away and looked at the front cover. "We have some Bibles here in our Sunday School room. Are you sure you want to give me this? It has your name on it."

"Yeah. I'm sure. Sorry it's a little used. There's a lot of pink highlighting in it. I guess it's good we like the same color. Maybe next time I come I can bring you a new one with your name on it."

What was I *saying*? The *next* time I come?

"Thank you for telling me about Jesus," Hannah said. "It was the best news I have heard in a long while."

I gave her a hug. "You're welcome. It's the best news you will *ever* hear."

"Oh, and thank you for the shoes. I will never forget yesterday."

I smiled, "Me either."

"Time to go!" Mom stuck her head out of the window of the matatu. "Come on, Riley. We're taking a quick trip into Eldoret before we head back to the village."

I climbed into the van and took a seat next to Faith, who had a book open.

"How's the studying going?" I asked.

"It is good now, since I am studying science and the human body. This lesson is about bones! It is amazing how God made all the parts to work together so well. I just hope I can learn all that I need to be a good doctor someday."

"You will. In fact, you'll be one of the best, I'm sure. Hey, guess what?" I said, "I think I know what God wants me to do when I grow up."

Faith slammed her book shut and looked at me. "What?"

"This."

Faith looked around. "He wants you to wear tight braids and bounce around in a matatu with African children?"

I laughed, "No. Well, maybe. If that's what it takes to spread his good news to kids who don't know about him."

"Oh," Faith raised her eyebrows. "So he wants you to be a missionary?"

"Yes. I mean, sort of. It's hard to explain, but yesterday was one of the most amazing days of my life. And it went by too fast!" I went on to explain to her how I shared the gospel with Hannah and how she and Fawn accepted Jesus into their lives.

Faith opened her book back up and smiled. "I understand completely. That is what happens when I study about the human body. The time flies by and I am filled with so much joy."

"That's so interesting! If anyone deserves to get into a good high school, it's you."

Faith's face turned serious. "But it is not guaranteed."

"Then we'll just ask Akeelah to pray harder for you."

"I will have her pray for both of us. Every morning. We will need it."

Chapter 41

The matatus rumbled to life and we rode away from Ruth's Village. I waved out the window to Aunt Wendi and Jonathan and to that really cool athletic kid Paul, and to Hannah. When she waved back, I spotted my Bible in her other hand. I smiled, turned around, and sat down.

"Yep," I said to Faith. "I'll definitely be back here someday."

Chapter 42

We arrived back in the village at sunset. As we stood and stared at the beautiful orange pinkness, Mom pulled me close and whispered in my ear, "I think our little African trip is coming to an end."

I got butterflies in my stomach. "Really? Are we going home?"

Mom smiled. "We're so close. We should have Eric in custody by tomorrow."

"In custody? Does that mean he's in trouble? Because I really don't think he's a bad guy."

Mom pulled on one of my braids, and tilted her head to look at me. "You are an amazing girl, do you know that? You've always trusted people. Very unlike me, that's for sure. I've always been a suspicious one, even when I was a kid."

"Well, God must have made you that way since he knew you would be a cop."

Mom crossed her arms. "Hmm, I suppose. I never thought about that before. I just thought there was some-thing wrong with me."

I shook my head. "Nuh uh. I've been thinking a lot about how God makes us all different. Look at Faith.

She's serious and determined and interested in science. She'll make a great doctor. Grace is silly and creative and makes up fun stories. I bet she'll be an author or something. I'm sporty and friendly and I ..."

I stopped for a minute.

Mom smiled, "You what?"

"Well, I just found out that I really like talking to people about Jesus."

Mom nodded. "See? I told you. You're amazing. You are following God's lead in your life and he will get the glory for it."

"Thanks, Mom." I hugged her. "Hey, do I have to go to school tomorrow?"

Mom laughed, "No. You can sleep in. We'll give poor Jomo a break."

"That sounds good," I said, "but if it's okay, I'd like to go to the prayer group and *then* come back and take a nap. Or have breakfast with you. Or maybe I'll work on those silly fan letters."

"Sounds like a plan," Mom said.

Chapter 43

No one had to wake me up the next morning. My eyes popped open and I checked my watch. Four forty-five. I pumped my fist in the air. "Yes!"

Then I reached over to shake Faith and Grace.

"Hey, you two, WAKE UP!" Then I started singing a goofy little song.

They both bolted up, looking like someone had thrown a cold bucket of water on them. Faith rubbed her eyes. "Riley," she said, "do you know that in the Bible, there is a verse that says that a lively greeting too early in the morning will be taken as a curse?"

"Oops!" I put my hand over my mouth. "I'm sorry," I whispered.

Faith smiled.

"I guess I'm just excited that I finally woke up before you guys. You wanna go to the prayer meeting?"

"Of course," Grace said. "We are still praying for you and Prince Sean to get together."

"Grace, as much as I appreciate that, remember I'm only thirteen. There's plenty of time for that."

"Not if Morgansithor is loose in the kingdom!"

Faith hit Grace with a pillow and then jumped out of bed. "Grace, you should focus on prayers for our brother."

"I have been praying for Sunday every minute," Grace said, and then she frowned. "I miss him and want him to come home."

"I do too," I said. "Let's go pray about it."

The prayer meeting went great. I shared with Akeelah that I wanted her to pray about me being a missionary when I grow up.

She chuckled. "But, my dear," she said, "you already are!"

"Well, you know what I mean," I said.

"Yes, I do. And I will pray about it every day."

"I believe you will."

After we left Akeelah's hut, Faith jetted off somewhere and Grace and I went into the hut. I pulled out my mailing envelope full of fan letters and asked Grace for help with the letter to Jessica—the girl who wanted to know if she should try a hike to the top of Half Dome even though she was afraid of heights.

"Well, what do you think?" Grace asked. "Should she try it?

"Well, of course she should," I said.

"But why?" Grace stared at me, blinking her eyes, waiting to write down what I would say.

"Well, it would be a challenge, that's for sure— especially if she's afraid of heights. But when she gets to the top, she will be amazed by the view, and she'll feel like she really accomplished something. She will have conquered her fear and that will help her have confidence to do the next hard thing that comes her way."

Grace tossed the notebook my direction. "You do not need me! That was the perfect answer."

"You really think that was okay? I mean, I've never thought of myself as a writer before."

Grace laughed, "I do not think it has anything to do with writing."

"I suppose you're right. But some of the questions are hard. Like this letter from Sarah. Her dad only wants to spend money for her brothers to play sports. What should I tell her?"

"Pretend I am Sarah. Say something to me."

"Well, okay." I cleared my throat and felt kind of weird. "Sarah," I said, as I looked in Grace's eyes and gave her a goofy look, which made her laugh some more. But then I got serious. "Sarah, tell your dad that playing sports gives you a chance to be physically healthy and to learn to work with a team of people. It also teaches you how to handle the challenges of losing without giving up and winning without becoming too proud. Those are things that girls need to learn just as much as boys."

"Wow!" Grace said. "You really are good at this."

I scratched my head. "I am?"

"Yes. You have many experiences you can share with girl athletes."

"I guess. Thanks to this crazy shoe contract, I've learned a lot lately. Ha! I never know what's going to happen next."

"I guess only God knows those things." Grace smiled.

Just then, we heard a bunch of noise outside. It sounded like girls yelling or crying or something.

We cracked open the door of the hut and looked out. A crowd of the older girls were gathered in the circle, looking worried.

Grace and I ran out to them.

"It is Faith!" one of them cried. "She came with us to carry water, and she was up on the road, ahead of our group ..."

Kiano, Akeelah, Fawn, and Mom had come out by this time.

Grace and I looked around, but did not see Faith.

"What happened?" I asked. "Where is she?"

"We do not know," another girl said. "We heard her scream, and then we heard an engine roar off. We think someone took her!"

My heart started beating hard in my chest. *No! Who would take Faith?*

Kiano ran into the men's hut and after a couple seconds Jomo, Flip, and Jomo's three big sons came running out. Jomo jumped on the boda boda and rode off with one of the sons riding on the seat behind him. The other two jumped into one of the trucks I thought was just junk. It sputtered at the start, but eventually they took off in it.

"Where are they going to look?" Fawn asked Kiano.

"All the neighboring villages," he replied. "And I will go on the road, toward town. We will stop at Ruth's Village first and then make our way into Eldoret to get help."

"We're coming too," Mom said.

"You will need supplies in case you are gone long," Akeelah said. "Come and I will pack some for you."

We followed Akeelah into her hut and she quickly prepared some food items and packed first-aid supplies.

"Is there anything else we should bring?" I asked Mom.

"Riley, you're NOT coming. You and Grace stay here with Akeelah."

"But Mom—"

"NO arguing! You're staying here."

"Grace," Akeelah said. "Please go tell Masara what is happening. She will need to take care of you girls and Hope for a while."

"Okay." Grace shot out the door and disappeared.

Next, Kiano burst in the door of Akeelah's hut.

"We will take the farming truck," he said to Mom. "It has bigger tires and will be able to go off-road if we need it. Meet me out there in five minutes."

He was holding a rifle.

I knew what I had to do, so I bolted out the door before anyone could stop me. I ran toward the women's hut in case anyone was watching, so they would think I was going to find Grace. Then I snuck behind it and ran back around to the small farming truck. I jumped onto the flat bed and crouched down between a bale of hay and the back of the cab and covered myself with a tarp. Almost immediately, I heard a group of people running toward the truck. I looked around for something to hold onto, but there was nothing within reach.

Uh-oh.

People jumped into the truck and slammed doors. The engine rumbled to life and backed up over some bumps onto the "sort of" road. I pushed my hands into the hay bail and grabbed some of the straw, hoping it and the weight of the tarp would keep me from falling off the flatbed truck. At first, when we were on the smoothest part of the road, it worked.

* * *

We bumped along, going straight for what seemed like fifteen minutes. My hands were getting scraped up, but at least I wasn't going anywhere. I relaxed for a minute, and let go of the hay to examine my scratched hands. But then, the truck swerved sharply and dipped to the right. I slid out from under the tarp, right off the flatbed, and into a heap on the ground.

"OUCH!" I rolled a bit down an embankment. When I stopped, my knees and elbows felt like they were on fire.

I heard the truck screech to a halt and the doors open and slam shut.

"RILEY! Is that you?" Mom ran down the embankment, followed by Flip and Fawn. "Are you okay?"

I stood and brushed myself off a little. "Yeah, I think, uh ... ow. Maybe." I bent my right arm and raised it to look at my elbow.

"Road pizzas. That's gotta hurt." Flip shook his head and pointed to my mashed-up knees. "What are you doing here, kiddo?"

"I told you to stay back in the village!" Mom shouted.

"I'm sorry. I just, I dunno. I wasn't thinking. We just HAVE TO find Faith!" I was practically shouting back. "She can't marry some mean old village guy. She's supposed to be a doctor!"

Fawn stood there with a determined look on her face and her arms crossed. "We'll find her. Don't you worry."

Fawn and Mom helped me climb back up the hill toward the truck. Kiano's eyes practically bugged out of his head when he saw me.

"I'm sorry, Kiano," Mom said, "but we have to take Riley back to the village."

"No," Kiano said. "Every second counts if we are going to find my daughter. She will have to come with us."

Mom nodded. "You're right." Then she turned to me. "You'll have to crunch in."

Inside the truck, Mom wiped my knees with some antiseptic and patched them with some bandages that Akeelah had sent. "I didn't think we would need these for you," she said.

"I'm really sorry."

Flip turned around from the front seat. "Don't bleed on the premium upholstery."

I looked around. There were a few holes and the rest of the seat was threadbare.

Our first stop was a small village, a little like the one where Kiano and his family lived. But this one was really run down, and the people didn't appear joyful at all. A grouchy-looking man told us he hadn't seen Faith, but that he had seen a young mzungu man with light curly hair driving a vehicle the day before.

"Must have been E-rock," Flip said.

I threw my hands up. "Okay, so is anyone going to tell me who E-rock is?"

"It's Eric," Fawn said. "That was his nickname when he was a kid."

I couldn't believe what I was hearing. "You know, I'm

getting pretty tired of everyone having another name. It's very confusing."

"You should talk, Mae Kiplabat." Flip held a water bottle over the seat. "Thirsty?"

I opened the bottle and drank down the fresh, clear water. When I swallowed, I realized that I had a bunch of dirt in my mouth from the fall. I imagined that this was what the water tasted like for most of the people who lived in the villages here. *Yuck*.

"Where are we going next?" I asked.

"Ruth's Village," Kiano said. "At least they have seen what Eric looks like, and they have vehicles and modern technology to help."

"I still don't understand why Eric would be here and why he would take Faith."

"That makes two of us," Fawn said.

We pulled into Ruth's Village, and Wendi and Jonathan came out immediately to greet us. Their smiles turned to frowns as soon as we announced our reason for coming.

"E-Rock came back here last night," Jonathan said. "He told us that he took extra time off work so he could stay and help work more on the building project."

"Where is he now?" Mom scanned the surroundings.

Jonathan shrugged. "Don't know. He asked to borrow a truck for an errand, and then he took off. I haven't seen him since early this morning."

"Okay," Mom said. "Can Riley stay here with you guys? And I'd like to borrow your phone and Internet so I can alert some people. Oh, I also need to get into Eldoret. Can I borrow one of your vehicles?"

"Of course," Wendi said. "This way. And Riley, the kids are in the courtyard right now, on their mid-morning break. You are welcome to join them. Hannah will be so excited to see you. She's been reading the Bible you gave her non-stop."

We all split up, though I didn't want to. Mom jogged to one truck and Kiano, Fawn, and Flip returned to the one we came in. I watched them speed off and I said a little prayer for everyone before turning toward the courtyard. I found Hannah, and we had a super-fun conversation about the book of John. Before I knew it, a bell rang, calling everyone in for lunch.

Hannah rubbed her belly. "Hamburgers today. Wanna race to the lunchroom?"

"Sure."

I watched Hannah take off toward the door wearing her Pink Flash running shoes. I started to follow her, but then I stopped short.

Over to the right of the dining hall, I noticed someone with a blond curly head of hair closing the curtains of the guest house kitchen window.

Chapter 44

And then the courtyard was empty of people. I ran toward the guest house and looked around. No vehicles anywhere and no sign of Wendi or Jonathan. I wasn't sure what to do. Should I yell, or go into the dining hall where everyone was enjoying their lunch and cause a scene? By then, the person under that blond curly head might escape. And I had to save Faith! I walked toward the back door of the guest house and turned the handle. The door was unlocked. I stepped in, and headed toward the kitchen, but ran into someone in the living room.

It was Eric.

"Oof! Oh. Sorry. Um ... Hello," I said. Adrenaline must have been squirting out my ears. And I felt dizzy with fear.

"Riley? What are you doing here?"

"I'm hiding from you! But obviously I'm not doing a very good job of it. What are *you* doing in Africa?"

"I'm looking for my brother and sister."

"That's what you said in Fresno after Flip's accident on Half Dome. But then bad things happened, so I don't believe you anymore. What are you *really* doing here?"

He sat on the chair across from the large sofa. "I have some explaining to do."

"No kidding."

"Look—I'm really not a bad guy. I just made some horrible decisions a long time ago and now I'm paying the consequences. And so are you. I'm trying to put an end to it, once and for all."

I didn't feel dizzy anymore, but my heart was still pounding in my chest. I didn't want to let on that I was afraid, so I calmly walked over to the sofa, sat down, and crossed my arms.

"Go ahead. Explain."

Eric stood up and began pacing and looking out the window.

"Where's Faith?" I asked.

"Faith?"

"Yeah. Sunday's sister. The girl you took."

"I didn't take anyone!"

"I don't believe you."

"Look. I told you, I'm not a bad guy."

He sighed. "Okay. A few years ago, I got involved with some guys who wanted to steal Dad's company."

Eric began pacing again.

"I was only seventeen, and I was jealous of Flip and Fawn because they had good jobs working for Dad, but I had to live in Colorado with my mom and finish college before Dad would hire me. So some of Dad's board of directors approached me and told me they could give me a large piece of the company when I turned eighteen if I gave them some information and signed a few papers—stuff like that. So I did it. I know it was stupid, but you have to believe me. I didn't know they were going to kill my dad!"

"I thought they all went to jail."

"They did, except for one that I know of. He's our lawyer, and Flip and Fawn still trust him for some reason. He pretends to be loyal to our family, but then he pays desperate people like my friend Drew to cause a bunch of accidents so he can continue to hurt Flip and Fawn and destroy Swiftriver."

"So Drew really was the one who threw the rocks on Flip?"

Eric nodded. "Yes. He confessed to doing it one day when he came to visit me at the ranch."

I jumped up on my feet. "Wait. Did this happen down by the barn? Was Drew driving a motorcycle?"

"Yes. How did you know?"

"I was looking for cookies that I left in your Jeep. I saw you two arguing, so I hid. Of course, I didn't know who Drew was at the time."

It was quiet for a moment. My head was spinning. Something didn't make sense.

"If he's your friend, why would he try to kill Flip?"

"We haven't been on good terms since we graduated high school and he got into drugs. That addiction has a strong hold on him, and he needs money. But even though we haven't been friends for a while, he told me that he wanted the backpack to *miss* hitting Flip. Drew's plan was to follow it up with a note telling Flip and Fawn that their cover was blown and to close Swiftriver or else. Unfortunately, Flip got a direct hit."

Eric started to say something else, and then stopped.

"What?"

He closed his eyes and looked down. "Drew also told me that he tampered with the plane, knowing that we would land safely because Tyler is a skilled pilot. And then he asked *me* for a large sum of money to stop whatever accident might happen next. Can you believe that? He collected money from our lawyer to scare my family, and then he had the nerve to ask me for money to *stop* him from scaring them. That's what he was doing that day at the barn. I turned him down."

I was suddenly really mad. Tears formed in my eyes. "Why didn't you tell the police? My mom was right there in Montana. You could have told her before Drew knocked Matt into the river! We could have all died, Eric!"

"I know. And I'm so sorry. I was trying to protect my reputation, and I was even trying to find a way to get Drew out of this mess. But it was a mistake. One of several I've made all along the way. I tried following Drew everywhere he went after that, to prevent another accident. He got away from me that day and when I saw what happened in the river, and that you all survived, I took off so I could have some time to figure out what to do."

"I can't believe you ran away. We thought you were holding the other end of that volleyball net."

Eric shook his head. "I'm very sorry, Riley. I didn't have time to stay and explain. I had to follow Drew. When he finally settled down for a couple of days in Colorado, I contacted your mom's police station in Clovis and anonymously gave them information that led to his arrest."

"Well, that was a good decision at least."

"Then I decided that the best thing was to find you guys and confess my part in everything and ask for forgiveness."

"How did you find us in Kenya?"

"A couple of weeks after the accident, I broke into Chuck and Carmie's house and I saw a copy of your travel itinerary."

"You *broke in* to those nice people's house?"

"I know. I'm horrible! And when I saw you were going to Kiano's village, I joined up with a missions team, and booked a flight on a regular airline so I could come over here and not look suspicious. Riley, I hope you'll believe me. I never wanted to see anyone get hurt. I love my brother and sister. But yes, I'm guilty of lots of terrible things. Greed, dishonesty, selfishness, stupidity."

"You forgot trespassing."

Then I remembered that I had been doing my share of breaking in and snooping too.

"You're right. I'm pretty messed up."

I sighed, and was quiet for a minute. "Not any worse than the Ninevites."

"The *what?*"

I shook my head, "Never mind."

Eric continued to pace and look out the window. I sat there and contemplated what I should say to him. The story of Jonah and the Ninevites popping into my head made me wonder if I was supposed to share the good news with Eric. I didn't really want to. After all, this guy almost got me killed in a Montana river!

And then I remembered that Faith was missing, and

probably in danger somewhere. Yes, Eric needed to hear the good news, but it would have to wait until I found my friend. I walked over and got eye to eye with Eric.

"So tell me the truth. Did you kidnap Faith?"

"No. I didn't. That's the absolute truth."

The adrenaline kicked in again. "Then you need to come with me to find her, right now!"

I grabbed Eric by the sleeve and pulled him out of the house.

"Do you have a truck?" I asked.

"Yeah, it's hidden down by the softball field. I've been using it to go to the different villages to look for you guys."

We ran like crazy down to the field. "Did you get any weird vibes from any of the villages you visited?"

"Yeah, most of them. They didn't like seeing a white man, that's for sure."

"No. Think, Eric! Which one was the weirdest?"

"Actually, there was one village not far from here. The guy wasn't just weird, he was mean. And now when I think about it, he seemed suspicious. Come on. I'll show you."

Chapter 45

We hopped into the truck and were on the road already when I had to kick myself. WHAT was I doing? I had no idea what to do if we ran into the guy who stole Faith. What was I going to do, ask him nicely to give her back and expect he'd do it just because I was a determined mzungu girl with flaming orange running shoes?

Never going to happen. So I did the best thing I knew to do. I prayed.

Dear God,

I'm in a crazy mess. Please help me not to do anything else stupid!

And please help us find Faith. And help us not to die in the process.

Amen.

And God answered fast. Because coming the other way on the road was the flatbed truck that I had fallen off of earlier. The one that now held Kiano, Flip, and Fawn. And Kiano's rifle.

"Stop the truck!" I yelled. And Eric stopped. I opened the passenger door and jumped out in front of the truck, waving wildly.

Flip and Fawn got out of the truck, but Kiano stayed in the driver's side.

"Riley! What are you doing here?" Fawn looked around.

"That doesn't matter right now. I think I know where Faith is!"

Flip shielded his eyes from the sun and squinted up at my driver. "Who are you with? Jonathan?"

I grabbed Flip by the shoulders and tried to get my breathing under control. "No. Flip, you've GOT to trust me on this. My driver is Eric, your brother."

Fawn gasped. She started toward the truck, but I grabbed her arm to stop her.

"He knows where Faith is."

Flip ran over to Eric's driver-side window. "E-rock? Is it really you?"

"Yeah, bro. It's me."

"Okay, then," Flip shook his head. "I'm very confused, but I'm gonna trust the shoe girl. Lead the way."

Eric started up the truck and Flip jumped in to ride with us. Fawn joined Kiano who turned his truck around and we all sped as fast as we could back to the run-down village where Eric had seen that mean man. As we pulled closer, I realized I had seen him too. Only this time, he had some nasty-looking friends standing next to him.

They approached our vehicle. The meanest guy looked like he was limping. "We have not seen your daughter," he said to Kiano. "Now take these mzungus and leave before there is trouble."

The guy was lying, I just knew it. I wanted to jump

out of the truck and run past them and start searching through their huts.

Out of the passenger-side window I spotted a frightened-looking older woman sitting on the ground in front of a hut, holding a chicken. Her eyes seemed to be looking in my direction. I squinted at her, pointed to myself, and mouthed the words, "Are you talking to me?"

She nodded.

She let go of the chicken and made some motions with her hands. First, she formed the shape of a woman, then pushed downward with her hand. Then she made a running motion with her fingers and pointed in a direction away from the village.

I knew what she meant. Faith had been here, but she ran away.

I pulled on Flip's shirt. "Guys, we gotta go. Now."

"Hang on, Riley. I think Kiano's getting through to them."

"NO. We can't wait. Faith went that way." I pointed away from the huts.

"What?" Flip's eyes got wide. "Did you see her?"

"No, but that woman did. We have to go after her!"

Eric must have heard everything I said, because he started the truck and we screeched out into the brush.

The bumping was ridiculous. I grabbed the door handle to keep my head from slamming into Flip's.

"She's a really fast runner, so she could be just about anywhere by now," I said.

"We'll find her," Flip said.

"We'd better, before a lion does."

Chapter 46

Seconds later, we heard the farming truck holding Kiano and Fawn roar up behind us. We slowed down so our windows could meet up.

Fawn stuck her head out the passenger window and yelled over to Eric, "Mind telling us where we're going?"

"Riley says that Faith ran this way."

The farming truck sped ahead of us. The big tires flicked rocks and brush up onto our window.

Flip laughed, "I didn't know that truck could go more that twenty-five miles per hour."

"I'm pretty sure it can't," Eric said.

Flip pushed hard on Eric's knee. "Well, step on it, bro!"

We caught up and continued to follow Kiano in the flatbed. We bumped and thumped through the brush for what seemed like forever. I looked one way, and then the other, and all I saw was grass and those crazy trees that I still didn't know the name of.

I wanted to cry, but I held it in. "How are we going to find her?"

"I'm sure Kiano is driving back in the direction of his village," Flip said. "He knows his way around."

"But does Faith?" I tried to think if I could find my way

home in Fresno if I was abandoned a few miles out on a country road. I didn't know.

The truck bumped again, and we caught air. Eric's and Flip's heads hit the roof of the truck.

"Dude," Flip said to Eric. "Are you trying to take me out, once and for all?"

"Flip, you gotta believe me, man. I've been trying to protect you."

Just then Kiano's truck skidded to a halt. Eric slammed on the brakes, and this time our heads whipped forward and almost hit the windshield. We came within inches of rear-ending the flatbed. Kiano's arm reached out from the truck and he pointed toward two of those mystery trees. I caught my breath when I looked in between them. There was Faith! She was standing with her arms stretched forward, and her hands bent upward.

"Let me out." I crawled over Flip and pushed open the door of the truck.

"Riley, wait a minute."

I ignored Flip's suggestion and flew toward Faith. When I reached her she glared at me, shook her head, and put her index finger up to her lips.

Something was terribly wrong with this picture. I turned my head back to look for the grown-ups, but they were still in the trucks.

I heard growling. And then, I saw them near the tree on our right side. Two lion cubs, wrestling with each other, looking so cute and innocent, like the ones we saw on our safari.

Faith slowly pushed me toward the other tree and pinned me against the trunk. She turned around and covered me with her body.

"Faith," I whispered. "What's happening?"

She pointed out, away from the tree, toward an area covered with tall, golden-colored grass. It waved back and forth, but that was weird because there was no wind. I squinted ... was that really the grass moving?

No it wasn't. It was mama lion, and she was coming toward us.

Chapter 47

"Faith, what should we do?"

Kiptoo, the guy from the elephant orphanage came to mind.

Do not come face-to-face with a lion, that is what.

"Stay very still," Faith said. "Pray that the cubs go back to her."

I started to pray. But I didn't even get out "Dear Lord" before those little balls of growling fur trotted our way. They gnawed at each other's necks and flipped over and over, not realizing the peril they were putting us in.

The lioness moved closer, her eyes focused in on us. She was still quite a ways away, but she stopped and roared.

"That was her warning," Faith said. "Next, she will either back away or she will leap forward." Faith looked over at Kiano, who was now out of his truck, with his rifle aimed at the lion.

Faith muffled a sob, "No ... please. Do not kill it."

Then she began to sing softly in another language. It sounded like one of the songs we sang at the prayer meeting.

The cubs stopped wrestling and one of them ran back

to the lioness. The other one tilted his head to the side and looked at Faith with rascally eyes.

"No," Faith shook her head. "Go to your mama, little Simba. Go on. Asante sana ... Mungu akubariki ..."

Kiano took a few steps closer to the lioness. He looked ready to pull the trigger.

"No," Faith whimpered.

I drew in a huge breath and held it.

And at that moment, the little lion cub turned and trotted back to his mama.

Kiano pointed his rifle in the air—fired—and the family of three bolted and disappeared into the high grass.

I blew out my breath and Faith and I crumbled to the ground—shaking, crying, hugging. In seconds, two sets of adult hands grabbed us. Kiano and Flip carried us and sat us on the back of the flatbed truck.

Fawn opened some bottles, poured cool water on rags and wiped our faces. She gave us the rest of the water to drink. "Faith, I'm so glad you're all right. What happened?"

Faith took a big sip of water and then wiped her mouth. "That awful man grabbed me from the trail while I was carrying water. He told me his village was a mess and he was going to take me to work and clean and cook for him." Faith scrunched her eyebrows. "He was mistaken."

"That must have been so scary!" I said. "How did you get away?"

"I stomped on his metatarsals with my Sole Fires,"

Faith smiled and lifted her foot to show off the shoes. "It is a good thing I did not choose to go barefoot today."

I scratched my head, "His metatarsals?"

"The bones on the top of his foot. I am pretty sure I broke a few. He will be limping for weeks."

I shook my head. "You are amazing, Faith. So tough and brave."

"No," she said. "Just determined, like you."

"I guess so. Hey, what did you say to that lion cub? Was it Swahili?"

"Did I talk in another language? I did not realize. Let me think … I said, "Go back to your mama, lion. Thank you very much. God bless you."

"Wow. Well, it worked! We'll have to remember to tell Kiptoo at the elephant orphanage what you said if we ever see him again."

I wiped the back of my hot, sweaty neck with the wet rag. "You know what? It finally feels like Africa around here. Do you think we could find some shade?"

Kiano pulled the flatbed up under one of those trees.

"Ah … that's much better. By the way, what *are* these trees called?'

"Acacias," Kiano said.

"Well, guess what? I love them. I wish we had some in Fresno."

"Hey, look!" Flip pointed to the top of the acacia tree, where some branches were shaking around. A brown creature stared down at us and made some grunting noises.

"Is that a monkey?" I stood up on the flatbed to get a better look. "It is! Finally! Flip, where's your camera?"

Flip held his hands up. "In all the hurry, I left it back in the village."

"That figures. Rats!" I put my hands on my hips. "Now how am I going to prove that I actually saw a monkey in Africa?"

Right then, a stream of liquid began to pour down on me. It landed on my shoulders first, then ran down my arms, dripping off my fingers. I jumped out of the flow, screaming.

"Is that PEE? Did that monkey just PEE ON ME?" I jumped around and wiped my hands on my pants. "That is SOOOO GROSS!" I heard squealing and more grunting from the tree, but I didn't look up. I never wanted to see a monkey in the wild *ever* again.

Everyone was laughing, Flip the loudest. And for that, I cleaned my hands off on his shirt.

"You know, I think I've had enough of Africa," I said. "Do you think you could get your jet out here soon and take us all home?"

"I think that could be arranged."

Chapter 48

The flights back to Fresno seemed longer than ever. Eric needed a flight back, so he traveled with us in the jet, and since he did have a lot of explaining to do, he spent most of the time huddled in the back seats with Flip and Fawn. There had been a lot of crying and hugging going on back there. Thankfully they didn't ask me to join them. I didn't need any more drama than was already taking place in my own heart and mind. I'd been trying to process it all the last hour or so while throwing a pink and purple softball up and catching it in my glove.

"Are you excited, Riley?" Mom sighed and plunked herself down in the seat next to me. "We're almost home." She looked more refreshed than I'd seen her in weeks.

"Yes," I tried to sound enthusiastic, but it was tough since I had to swallow a big lump in my throat.

Mom reached out and put her arm around me. "What's wrong, honey?"

"I dunno. I feel weird." I threw the softball up and caught it again and turned my head to look back at Flip, Fawn, and Eric. "Are they gonna be okay?

"They'll be fine. Much better now that the truth is out and they can all deal with it."

"Do they still get to be Swiftriver?"

"I don't see why not. I mean, as long as they want to." Mom elbowed me in the ribs. "They have a contract with you, you know."

I tossed the softball again and smiled, "Yeah. And I'm not letting them out of it. I know this sounds crazy, but after all we've been through together, they're kinda like family. Life would be sort of boring without them now."

Mom chuckled, "Well, I for one would like things to slow down just a *little*."

Our trustworthy pilot, Tyler, came over the intercom.

"Good afternoon, folks! I hope you are enjoying your flight on Swiftriver Airlines today. And speaking of rivers, I thought you might like to take a look out the right side of the aircraft. That big hole you see is called the Grand Canyon, and the body of water flowing through it is the Colorado River. If you ever want to experience a thrilling raft trip, the Colorado River offers challenging rapids and breathtaking views."

I rolled my eyes. "I think I'll pass."

Tyler continued. "I would also like to inform you that we will be arriving at Fresno Yosemite International Airport in approximately one hour. Once again, thank you for flying Swiftriver Airlines, and I hope that you'll choose us again for your next Riley Mae adventure."

"Oh, I'm so excited. I can't wait to see your dad and brother." Mom got up and began to gather some things up toward the front of the jet.

I unzipped my backpack and shoved my glove and ball in. As I did, I heard some papers crunch, and I remembered that I had put Dad's letter in there for me to finally look at on the way home. I pulled everything back out, opened the scrunched envelope and tried to flatten the paper out on my knee as I began reading.

How's my girl?

Yep. That's as far as I got last time before I almost lost it.

Riley, there's not a day that goes by when I don't miss you and think about how much I love you. You're the best daughter any dad could ever hope to have! I am so proud of the way you've handled all the difficulties surrounding Swiftriver shoes. I think back on how we prayed to ask God if he wanted us to sign that contract—if the job would be part of his good plans for you. And I wonder if we would have still signed it if we knew that you'd end up in Africa, hiding from bad guys!

   I've been praying even more since you've been away, and I still believe we did the right thing. Even though we don't yet know how it will turn out, even though we're not sure when you are coming home. God is good, and he will use all of this to shape you into the wonderful young lady he wants you to be. You'll see! So keep on looking to him, Riley. He is with you wherever you go, whether it's in Montana or Africa, or wherever is next (and I hope it's Fresno).

Love you, Dad

The last hour of the flight flew by and soon I was staring out the jet window at our flat little city of Fresno. And my stomach jumped because I thought for a minute that I actually saw my house!

Dad and Brady were waiting inside a private little room at the airport. We all sort of piled into a big family hug. It lasted awhile, and we all kissed each other and cried a little, except my brother. He seemed happy though. Finally, after a couple of minutes, he wriggled away and said, "Okay, I'm good now." We all laughed when Brady asked, "So now can we get that puppy?"

Mom ruffled his hair and put her arm around him as they began to walk out to the parking lot. "We're going to need a few good nights of sleep first. But then we'll talk."

Dad's tears were the last ones to dry up. He hugged me real tight, then put his hands on my shoulders and looked into my eyes.

"How's my girl?" he said.

"Well, I—"

"Riley, I'm so *sorry* I wasn't there with you. Mom told me about the race, and how you went to a village school, and about the elephant … and then the lion! I would have been there to protect you if I could."

"Dad—"

"I prayed every day that you would be healthy."

"Hey, it worked. I didn't even get traveler's diarrhea!"

He laughed, "Well, that's a big relief." He hugged me again. "It's so good to see your face!"

"It's good to see yours too." I took my fingers and rubbed them on his whiskers. "And … I want you to know something."

"What?" He rubbed his face and gave me funny look.

"I just want you to know … I'm so glad you're my dad."

He smiled, "Me too."

Chapter 49

Fresno felt weird the day after I got home. As I stared out the window of our mini-van while Mom and I ran a million errands, I thought the town seemed smaller. And though there wasn't a cloud in the sky, the sun seemed dimmer. Maybe it had always been that way, but I just didn't notice.

But the next day, while we were running more mindless errands, the place brightened up considerably.

My phone rang.

"Hello? Is this my good friend, Miss Riley Mae Hart?"

"Sunday?"

"Yes, it is me! And I have good news."

"Sunday—you *are* good news! What? Are you getting better?"

"Well, almost. Or, probably not. Only God really knows about that. But I do know that I will be having my next treatments at a place near you."

"Where?"

"I am coming to Valley Children's Hospital in Fresno. Nurse Diane just transferred there, and she is the best, you know."

"Rusty's *mom* is moving to Fresno? That's amazing!"

I had to put my phone down and take a breath.

"Riley, are you still there?"

I brought the phone back up to my ear. "Yes. I'm still here. I'm just in SHOCK!"

"Well, I hope you are going to be okay, because I want you to be in good shape to show my sisters around Fresno when they arrive in a month. Mr. Flip is moving our whole family there."

Oh my. This was unbelievable!

Faith is going to get to go to a good high school! Lord, THANK YOU!

"Sunday, does Brady know about this?"

"Of course. He is my best friend. We have been talking about it every day for about a week."

* * *

I hugged my brother when we got home. Brady held his arms stiff to his sides while I did it, and after I let go, he narrowed his eyes and scanned back and forth across the room.

Then he looked back at me. "What was *that* for? Didn't we already do this the other day at the airport?"

"I don't know. I guess I just really missed you while I was in Africa."

He looked relieved and plunked down on the couch. "I wish I could have gone. It sounded adventurous. Hey, what ever happened to Gerald the alligator?"

"I decided to leave him there, so he could help protect the village kids. I'm sorry."

Brady smiled. "Good. Well, maybe we can name our new puppy Gerald."

"That would be great." I plopped down next to him. "Hey, Brady ..."

"Yeah?" He picked up the remote and pointed it at the TV.

I took it away from him and cleared my throat. "I've been thinking about something for a while now, and I want you to know that ... well, I'm going to try to be a better sister from now on."

He looked confused. "Why? I like you the way you are."

"Really? That doesn't make any sense! I'm impatient and I freak out way too much when you bug me."

"Sure you do. But that's my entertainment, you know. It's been boring around here lately with no one to react unfavorably to my antics."

"Oh."

Brady put his fist up to his chin and thought a minute, "But I'll try to bug you less, if that would make you feel better."

"I guess it might."

He grabbed the remote back from me.

"Okay, because I consider myself fortunate to have you for a sister. I mean, you really only have one major flaw."

I couldn't wait to hear what the genius fourth-grader was going to say.

"Oh really? And what is that?"

"You have waaaaay too many shoes."

Chapter 50

My best friend TJ was the first one to come by the house after I got home. She practically knocked me down when she ran to hug me.

"I missed you so much!" She stepped back and stared at me. "What in the world did you do to your hair?" She grabbed a braid and pulled. "Our whole team should get these!"

I rubbed my hand over the bumpy braids that my friends at the Kenyan school had worked so hard on.

"Actually," I said, "I was going to take them out tonight, but I'm a little afraid of what my hair will look like for church tomorrow."

TJ looked at me kind of funny. "I haven't been to church at all since you left."

"What? Why not?"

TJ shrugged. "Not sure. You know I had softball all those weeks. But we haven't had games the last two Sundays. I guess I felt like I needed a break, so I slept in and relaxed instead of going."

"But didn't you miss being at church?"

TJ rolled her eyes. "Not really. You weren't there, and there's that whole awkward decision to make about youth group."

I couldn't believe what I was hearing. I stepped back from TJ and sat down. "Do you know that when I was in Africa I woke up every morning to go to a prayer meeting at five o'clock?"

"Wow. That sounds horrible." TJ came and sat down.

"But it wasn't! Well, actually, at first I thought it was crazy. But then …"

"Let me guess—you fell asleep?" TJ laughed and slapped me on the back.

"No. After awhile I started to like it."

"Are you serious?" TJ scrunched her eyebrows together.

"TJ, I felt like I could hear God speak to me when I was in those meetings."

"Okay, now I know you're joking." TJ still looked confused. "Or maybe your braids are too tight."

"No, I'm not kidding. And God helped me share the good news of Jesus with a girl named Hannah."

TJ crossed her arms. "Well, I'm not at all happy you missed All-Stars. I guess we can say good-bye to the dream of having matching championship trophies as this year's co-MVPs."

"Huh?"

TJ stood. "Do you wanna come over tonight and hit pitches and make some brownies?"

I stared into the eyes of my friend. "You know I do."

"Cool." TJ jumped up off the couch. "See you later, then? We can take out the braids and see if your hair turns out looking like a lion's mane."

I shuddered. "Sure."

TJ seemed different too. Like Fresno. Not as bright and shiny as before.

And then a funny thought hit me.

Is my best friend a Christian?

And then I heard that deep-down whisper.

She needs me too, Riley.

Chapter 51

My hair turned out okay. TJ had some good conditioner, and with a little help from the straightener, it almost looked as good as normal. I even had a few new blonde highlights to show off.

I convinced TJ to come meet me in the parking lot of the church the next morning.

"So," I said, "are we going to kid's church or to the youth group with the scary boys with mustaches?"

Just then, someone came up from behind. "Hi, Riley."

The voice sounded familiar, but it was a little lower than I remembered, and it cracked in the middle of saying my name. I turned.

"Oh, hi, Sean."

"Hi."

I smoothed my hair a bit. "How are you?"

I could see how he was. Taller. And cuter than when I last saw him. I even liked the little bit of fuzz on his upper lip. How could that happen in just a couple of months?

"I'm good." His voice cracked again, and I tried not to laugh out loud. He held his right hand behind his back.

Please be a chocolate donut.

It was. "Did they have these in Africa?" he asked.

I grabbed it out of his hand and took a bite.

"Well, they had a few good things in Africa, but not anything like this."

Sean smiled, and our eyes locked. What seemed like only a moment later, a beautiful girl with long, straight, brown hair ran up to us.

"Sean, we're going to be late."

Sean pulled his phone out of his pocket and checked the time. "Oh, wow. Uh, hey, Riley … this is a new … uh … friend of mine. Morgan, Riley. Riley, Morgan."

Morgan crossed her arms and gave Sean a grumpy-looking stare. Then she turned from him, smiled at me, and held out her hand.

"It's nice to meet you, Riley. I've heard many nice things about you from everyone."

I held out my clammy hand to shake hers. "It's nice to meet you too."

"Are you coming to youth group today?"

Decision time.

"Are *you* going?" I asked.

She smiled, "Of course."

"Well then. I'd love to come."

"Well, we'll see you in there then." She grabbed Sean's hand. "Are you coming? I don't want to miss the worship band." She pulled a little, and then Sean turned and let her drag him toward the youth room.

"Hey," TJ nudged me with her elbow. "Did you forget I was here? I mean, I know he's cute and all."

I kept my eyes on the two as they moved closer to the room and walked in the door.

"Do you think she grabbed his hand to drag him over there, or do you think she was, you know, *holding* his hand?"

TJ shook her head. "I don't know, but we better go in there and see."

"Hey, Riley Mae Hart! Elephant whisperer! I have something to show you."

I turned to see Flip getting out of a car with his sister, Fawn, and Matt, our outdoor guide who was also Fawn's boyfriend now.

Flip ran over and shoved a computer printout into my hand. "Check this out," he said. "This will be in print next month."

It was a rough draft copy of my new question and answer column for *Outdoor Teen Magazine*. It was titled "Girls on the Move," and it included the letters from Jessica and Sarah and other helpful answers to letters that Grace and I wrote while I was in Africa.

"Let me see that." TJ took the paper from my hands and skimmed the article. "Wow, you're going to be even more famous now!"

"Of course she is," Fawn said. "And here are a few more letters for you to choose from for your next article." Fawn handed me a thick manila envelope.

"How am I going to do this, keep up with my Swift-river schedule, *and* finish my school work too?"

"You'll find a way," Fawn said.

"Hey," TJ said, "we need to get in there pretty soon."
She pointed to the youth room.

I frowned.

"What's the matter?" Flip said.

"TJ," I said. "Can you go in and save me a seat? I need
to talk to these guys for a minute."

TJ rolled her eyes. "Okay. But you better not chicken
out and leave me alone in there." She jogged off, and as
she opened the door, she glanced back and put her hand
to her forehead like she was going to faint or something.

"Now *why* would you chicken out of going to church?"
Flip asked.

"It's youth group! This is my first time going. I'm just a
little intimidated."

Fawn looked toward the door of the youth group
room. "Are you kidding me?"

"About what?"

"Come on, Riley! You've been to the top of Half Dome
in Yosemite, you've gone down a waterfall without a raft,
and you've been to Africa and survived in a primitive
village—all while bad guys have been chasing you and
putting your life in danger. What in the *world* could be
scarier than all that?"

I pointed toward the door. "Being a youth group
reject."

"You're afraid of rejection?" Flip said.

"Yeah," I said. "What if they don't like me? What if
they don't talk to me?"

"Well," Flip said. "We *could* arrange a trip to another
country. India, perhaps?"

I put my hand up. "Oh, no. You promised the next trip would be a vacation. Hawaii, remember? And I get to bring my friends. We're going to learn to surf!"

Tons of people were now jumping out of their parked cars and crowding the sidewalk on their way to the church service. A few of the people recognized me and waved.

"Hey, we better get in there so we can get a good seat," Matt said. "Maybe we can all do lunch together and you can tell us how things went in youth group, Riley."

"Sure." For some reason, a tear formed in the corner of my right eye.

"Hey," Fawn said. "You guys go on and I'll be there in just a minute."

Matt smiled and winked at Fawn. "Okay, see you in there."

Flip punched me in the arm. "Don't you worry, Shoe girl. I liked you from the minute I met you. They will too." Then he hugged me and walked off.

The tear escaped from my eye and traveled down my cheek.

Fawn took me by the arm and led me over to a bench near a tree.

"So," I said, "where's Eric? I hoped he might come to church today."

Fawn frowned. "He went back to Colorado for a while."

"Is everything okay?"

Fawn's eyes focused on her clasped hands in her lap. "Well ... no. It isn't. I just need some time to process everything before we can be a happy family again."

"But he apologized for everything. And you forgave him, right?"

"Of course. And I'm so relieved that he finally confessed and told us about our lawyer. That's one more awful person out of the way. I just hope there aren't anymore out there."

I shuddered at the thought of more Swiftriver drama. "So what's the problem then?"

Fawn shook her head. "I don't know. It's hard to put my finger on it. I'm still mad, or ... something. So much has happened. That's why I need some time. And Eric's been gracious enough to give it to me."

"Well, I'm glad you at least forgave him. You don't want to be like that prophet, Jonah. That guy was bitter!"

Fawn smiled and then gazed off in the distance. "I want you to know something. The day I met you was one of the most important days of my life."

I turned my head toward her and laughed.

"Really? That was a funny day! You and Mom fought over me wearing makeup, remember?"

"Yes, and I remember that I lost that fight."

"You were dressed horribly too."

"Ah, yes. The high heels and the white skirt."

"On a baseball field."

Fawn closed her eyes and grimaced. "Yes, that *was* horrible."

She turned to face me.

"I was a pretty lost person back then," she said.

"I thought you were super tough."

"Well, I acted tough on the outside, but on the inside I

was definitely broken. I was dealing with so many losses in my life—my mom, my dad, my step-family, my iden-tity. Riley, I was an orphan! It finally hit me that morning when we were praying with Masara. And I realized that I had no foundation, nothing of meaning to hold on to. I really needed Jesus, but for some reason, I kept shutting him out of my life. Oh, I knew Flip was a Christian, but..."

"Flip's crazy," I said. And we both laughed.

"Yep," Fawn said. "That he is. But then you came along, and you were a lot like I was when I was your age, except you were fun and honest and joyful—a breath of fresh air. You were really good news. You made me wish I could go back to that age and start over with Jesus."

"I'm glad I could help a little."

"Are you kidding? You helped a lot! And then, when I overheard you talking with Hannah at Ruth's Village, I knew it was time for me to take the step to finally let Jesus in. And he's already made a huge difference in my life."

Fawn grabbed me by the hand and we stood up together. She put her hands on my shoulders and looked me in the eyes.

"So go in that youth room and be yourself! God has plans to use you here, just as much as he used you in Africa. Don't let the fact that they're older than you, or that they're sitting here in a church fool you. I'm sure many of them are just as broken as I was, and they could use the good news that you have to share with them. Faith told me you want to be a missionary. Well, today this is your mission field."

She put on a serious face and pointed toward the youth room. "Now, go!"

"You're so bossy!" I smiled at Fawn, and then turned and walked toward the room.

I heard music coming from the inside. I took a big breath and opened the door.

I expected everyone to be looking my direction and gasping at the new weird girl. But no, they were all turned in the other direction, standing, facing the worship band. I scanned the room for TJ but couldn't see her shiny brunette head anywhere. It was probably being blocked by some of the monstrous boys sitting in the middle rows.

"Riley!"

I glanced over to the sound of the voice. It was Morgan. And she was motioning to an empty seat next to her. I squished by a couple girls to get to the seat.

"I saved this place for you," Morgan said.

Well that was nice of her. All of a sudden I felt bad that I had Grace name the dragon Morgansithor in her story.

Sean leaned back and tapped me on the shoulder. "Glad you made it," he said. His right eye twinkled a little.

It was nice to see that they were both clapping their hands and not holding each other's.

We sang one more song and then Pastor Mark led us in a prayer. He had a funny accent.

"He's from Australia," Morgan whispered.

We all sat down after that and then the discomfort began.

Pastor Mark, the "Aussie," held up a huge candy bowl.

"Hey, we're glad you're all here—especially our first time guests. We don't want to make you feel uncomfortable or anything, but if you would like to come up and introduce yourself, you can have all the candy you want out of this bowl."

The candy looked good, but I slumped down in my chair.

"Come on," Morgan said. "I'll go with you."

Rats. This girl was persistent. Maybe she *was* a dragon after all.

Pastor Mark looked excited. "Man, look at this group! I'm stoked! So, real quick, let's just have you introduce yourself and tell us a little bit about who you are. Then we'll leave you alone to go eat your candy."

I didn't go first. And I didn't hear a thing the other kids said. I just wanted to die. This was the one thing I had been dreading for years.

I closed my eyes and heard Fawn's voice in my head: *Today, this is your mission field.*

I opened my eyes, and Pastor Mark held out the candy bowl. "You look like a girl who loves chocolate." He smiled.

"You got that right." I grabbed the bowl.

"Cool. So tell us your name and a little bit more about yourself."

I took a deep breath and blew it out. I scanned the room, and finally found TJ in the second row. Why didn't she come up as a first-time visitor? Chicken! And then I noticed that Rusty was sitting next to her, smiling. And that made me smile.

I guess this was my moment.

I silently prayed: *God, help me wear the Good News Shoes. Right here, where I am.*

Then I opened my mouth.

"My name is Riley Mae Hart, and I have the best shoe collection of anyone you know. Not the dressy ones that pinch your toes. I'm talking about the shoes you can *do* stuff in—like hike, run, jump, and play sports. I have at least a hundred pairs. And they didn't cost me anything! Well, that's not exactly true. I *did* pay in sweat, scrapes, lots of tears, and a broken bone or two. I know—that sounds bad. But it's really not, I promise. In fact—looking back—I wouldn't change a thing ..."

Acknowledgements

There is simply no way I could have written this book without the help of many talented, loving, and godly people. Many thanks go to:

My husband, **Mike**—for praying for me and for holding my hand in the midst of this "cannonball." I love you!

Jen, Matt, Paul, and Katrina—for being the most amazing kids in the world, and for displaying all the positive traits that show up in all my characters!

My Life Group—for not rolling your eyes when every single week my prayer request was for help with this book!

Kim—for loving Riley Mae, and for your prayers. I will always thank our Good Shepherd for putting us together.

Alyssa—for encouraging me to keep wrestling with words until they were wonderful.

Charles—for sharing about your life growing up in Kenya. I admire your hard work and determination, and I will be praying for you and your lovely wife.

Everyone at Naomi's Village, Maai Mahiu, Kenya—for causing me to fall in love with the children of Kenya. Thank you for sharing their stories through your website, videos, and blogs, and for giving those precious children hope and a place to belong. I look forward to visiting soon and meeting the future leaders of Kenya!

The Smoking "Gunns"—my wonderful critique buddies. I wish you never-ending M&Ms!

Judy and Kathy—for being such fun Mount Hermon roomies and prayer partners. I loved our discussions at our dining room table in our "cabin of blessings."

Jesus—for everything. And for helping me wear The Good News Shoes!

And last but not least...

To the awesome young ladies (and anyone else) who will read these books—for being you! You are God's masterpiece. (See Ephesians 2:10.) You were designed by Him for a special purpose. No one can ever take your place! So, don't hold back. Put on your favorite shoes and go out and shine for Jesus! Contact me through Zonderkidz and let me know how I can help.

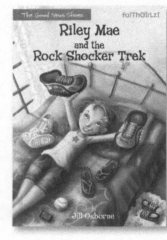

Faithgirlz!
The Good News Shoes

Riley Mae and the Ready Eddy Rapids

Jill Osborne

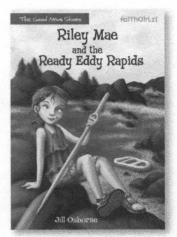

If you're gonna run for your life, you gotta wear the right shoes.

Life is rapidly changing for pre-teen shoe spokesperson Riley Mae. After the last photo shoot and trek up the Half-Dome in Yosemite, Riley Mae and her Swiftriver friends find themselves in Northwest Montana, the perfect backdrop for a river sandal campaign. The first problem is a plane malfunction. Then the rigorous raft training for the "Ready Eddy" river sandal campaign brings more bumps and bruises. And given that she is in Montana for a shoe campaign instead of back home with her friends, Riley thinks life can't get much worse. But then she meets Sunday, a 10 year-old boy from Kenya, who wrestles fish, battles bears, and tackles leukemia. And Riley soon learns that life is as unpredictable as the raging waters, which, if she is not careful, will sweep her away and into the hands of the enemy—who is even closer than she thinks.

Available in stores and online!